Archibald Forbes

Soldiering and scribbling

A series of sketches

Archibald Forbes

Soldiering and scribbling
A series of sketches

ISBN/EAN: 9783741174544

Manufactured in Europe, USA, Canada, Australia, Japa

Cover: Foto ©Andreas Hilbeck / pixelio.de

Manufactured and distributed by brebook publishing software
(www.brebook.com)

Archibald Forbes

Soldiering and scribbling

.

Soldiering and Scribbling.

A SERIES OF SKETCHES.

BY

ARCHIBALD FORBES.

LONDON:

HENRY S. KING & CO., 65 CORNHILL.

1872.

PREFACE.

THE papers which make up this little volume are, without exception, reprints. Some were originally contributed to the "Starlight" column of the now defunct *Evening Star*; others appeared in *St Paul's*, the *Daily News*, the *London Scotsman*—"gone dead" like the *Star*—the *Observer*, the *Sunday Magazine*, and *Belgravia*. To the proprietors of the living among the journals and periodicals named, I desire to make my acknowledgments for the permission accorded me to reprint. Whether the reader may or may not consider that a refusal on their parts of this permission would not have been true kindness, is a question on which I do not presume to advance an opinion. It may be necessary to state that, where the first person singular is used, it by no means follows that I am narrating my own experiences; but that the "I" was adopted for the sake of greater directness, and in the impression that a narrative told in the first person has the effect of greater realism.

But that person I never adopted without warrant for my facts. Thus I never was in a military prison, I never was flogged, and I never was a deserter ; but I know that the statements made in the papers bearing these headings are strictly true.

CONTENTS.

———

A PENNY A-DAY.

A PENNY A DAY.*

EXACTLY the sum, reader, which you contentedly set aside every day for the purchase of your *Daily News* or *Standard;* but how would you relish its being the magnificent sum-total of your diurnal spending-money? Whence would come cigars, gloves, opera-stalls, cabs, new novels, and the thousand-and-one et-ceteras which use has made necessaries? Nevertheless, this single copper represents the available day's cash for many a gallant dragoon, spite of all the fancied pleasures of his lot, with its conventional accompaniments of pretty girls in galore, beer in lashings, and nothing to do but cultivate moustaches. Nor for a day either, or even a week, but often for a month or two at a spell.

The swells at the War Office may laugh me to scorn, and assert that the dragoon's pay ought to be reckoned in silver, and not the baser metal, copper; but *experto crede*, I have soldiered for six months at

* This paper was written before the daily addition of 2d. was made to the private soldier's pay, at the instance of General Peel. No private soldier need now be on "a penny a day." In other respects, besides increased pay, there have been material ameliorations in his condition.

11

a stretch on a penny a day, and I claim to be considered a master in the art of " financing " under difficulties.   And how this depth of impecuniosity is reached may fall out in three ways.   First, the dragoon's pay is nominally 1s. 4d. per diem, out of which 9d. is deducted for rations, washing, &c., leaving the magnificent surplus of 7d. free for him to disburse as seemeth unto him good.   But out of this income he has to pay for all clothing except the Government tunic, overalls, and boots ; and as a jacket costs him 17s. 6d., a change of underclothing about 10s., and a cap nearly half as much, it will easily be seen that his task is no light one.   If he is careful, he can replace underclothing as it wears out without undergoing a stoppage of more than 2d. a day out of his 7d. ; but when his jacket gets dingy, and the inexorable colonel condemns it, there is nothing for him but to shoulder his cross in the shape of a penny a day till the 17s. 6d. is wiped out of the sergeant-major's account-book.

The second cause which reduces the dragoon to these "hard lines" is this.   He craves a furlough, or a day or two's leave of absence, and as to save sufficient money to pay the expenses of this indulgence is a practical impossibility, he is compelled to appeal to the captain of his troop for an advance.   This gentleman is mostly tender-hearted, and is no usurer.   He does not take interest, but to insure payment our bold holiday-maker, on his return from his trip, has to look a penny a day straight in the face till the advance is refunded.

The third cause is desertion, or, to be more accurate, recapture after desertion.   When the soldier contemplates a skedaddle, he, like the fraudulent bankrupt, proceeds to realise; and as his whole available property is his kit, he parts with it, *sub rosa*, for what it will fetch. Thus, being retaken, tried, and his imprisonment over, he faces the world again kitless, and, as an unfailing consequence, finds himself on a penny a day till he has paid for a new outfit, the price of which being somewhat about £6, it may be easily credited that some of the less durable articles require replacing before the cost of the whole has been paid—involving, of course, more debt, and more "penny a day." I have known a man on a penny a day for two years at a stretch from this cause; and I can remember a sergeant, who proved a defaulter to the tune of £50, reduced to the ranks, and sentenced to repay his deficit in a manner which involved his being on a penny a day till it was wiped out. He tarried till his hair was grown, which had been cropped to the bone in prison, and then he shook the dust of the regiment from off his feet, and, in the language of the barrack-room, "stepped it."

Having thus reduced our friend the dragoon to his penny a day, let us see how he sets about "financing," so as to make it satisfy his varied wants; a task which I fear would make Mr Lowe, in default of the surplus he is wont yearly to show, drown himself, with a Tory budget round his neck by way of a millstone. As I have said, an appreciative country finds him (the soldier, not the statesman) in return for 9d. a day, his rations, &c. These consist of tea, or coffee, twice a day, 1¼ lb. bread, ¾ lb. meat (*with* bone, and how soldiers' meat comes to have so much bone I think it worthy of the inquiry of Professor Owen),

and a fair supply of vegetables. This is not bad fare
so far as it goes ; but a penn'orth of butter helps the
dry bread down wonderfully, and commissariat bread
is dry, suggestive of sawdust to the contemplative
mind ; a bunch of water-cresses, a radish, or a bloater,
is a simple but agreeable relish : a pickle can trans-
form "old horse" into "young bullock," the modest half-
pint aids digestion, and a morsel of bread and cheese,
especially when a night on sentry is in front of a man,
is a frugal but invigorating supper. But the dragoon,
if he would have these, or any of these, must find
them out of his private pay, as we may term the 7d.
left him after the commissary is satisfied ; and there
are, besides, to quote the cry of the barrack-room
hawker, "soap, oil, blacking, chrome yellow, pipeclay,
and blue"—mysterious articles to the civilian, but
which the soldier must buy in the interest of his
accoutrements, and on which he ought to lay out, if
he wants to maintain a creditable appearance, at least
a penny every day. And last, but not least, there is
the soldier's darling solace, his pipe, to keep which
agoing will cost a moderate smoker three halfpence
a day. So it is abundantly apparent, that even on
what he triumphantly calls "full dig," the dragoon's
income is not far beyond his wants, and does not
leave a wide margin to be expended in the conventional debaucheries in which he is popularly, but most
erroneously, believed to wallow.

But at this rate you must exclaim, Heaven help
the poor devil on short pay, much more the wretch
on a "penny a day !" Nevertheless, he is in what
Captain Truck would have called the "category ;"
and so he sits down with us at his elbow to look his

position fairly in the face. First, then, he perforce
takes the pledge, for even such a bagatelle as half-a-
pint of beer would swallow up his penny, and he is
miserably conscious that the brief pleasure would cost
him too dear. He can't give up the pipe, but he husbands the "dottle" religiously, counts the number of
"draws" he takes, has a whiff seldomer, and when
fairly stumped throws himself on the generosity of his
comrades. As for relishes and butter, they are as
much out of his reach as a field-marshal's baton, and
he munches his dry "toke" with an appetite which,
to do a soldier's life justice, is seldom wanting. Supper he is compelled to abjure, "taking it out in sleep,"
like the funny debtor in "Pickwick," and is in the
arms of Morpheus when his more fortunate mates
are eating their bread and cheese, or picking their
ham-bones. He "forages" for cleaning utensils, soap,
oil, &c.—that is to say, cadges off raw recruits; sometimes, I fear, invades a neighbour's stable-bag when
his back is turned; and if reduced to the last ex-
tremity, goes without, and stands the racket of a
blowing-up for being dirty.

He is always profuse in his offers to do anything for
anybody by which a copper can be picked up, and will
clean a saddle, or get a man who is in funds ready for
parade with extraordinary alacrity, working with good
will a couple of hours for as many pence. He is particularly attentive to recruits before their bounty is
exhausted, volunteering to initiate them into the complete art of soldiering, and realises many a sixpence
and many a pot of beer (not without earning the
same) off those specimens of unfledged men-of-war.
He is always willing to be the agent for the disposal

of any article any gentleman may be desirous of
selling, and hawks it from room to room with amus-
ing pertinacity, in the hope of obtaining a trifle more
than the limit fixed by the owner, as his own perqui-
site.   And then he has a chum—for a true comrade
will not desert his *fidus Achates* because he is in reduced circumstances, the lot may be his own to-
morrow.   It is hard indeed if both are on short pay
at once, and the one never wants what the other has ;
yet a spirit of sturdy independence is often developed,
and I have known a man cease chumming with another when he found himself unable to contribute
equally to the joint-treasury.

   If our friend lose heart in his trouble, and there
be a green doctor in charge, he has still another
resource—he goes into hospital.   "What !" you
ask, "without a disease ?"   Ay, if need be ; or
he makes one for the occasion.   A "bad chest,"
"palpitation of the heart" (easily induced by a
short course of soap-pills and pipeclay-water, or
by perseveringly knocking the elbows against a wall
for half-an-hour before entering the surgery), or "the
pains" are never-failing ailments ; and a doctor must
have had some experience of the service to look a
man in the face, and call him a liar, when, with a
face like a coffin-lid, he tells him he has a "terrible
tightness across the chest," or "awful pains in the
bones, sir."   Once admitted into hospital, he luxuri-
ates on hospital comforts and the pleasure of doing
nothing, while his debt is going on diminishing ; and
his recovery is apt to bear a curious coincidence in
time with the period of his reinstatement on full
pay.

The dragoon, indeed, while in the state of abject poverty represented by a "penny a day," may be said to vegetate rather than enjoy life, or it may not be far-fetched to say that he hybernates, until the winter of his discontent is passed, and the glorious summer of full pay returns.

But when he is enterprising, and not particularly scrupulous, he sometimes essays to carve out of the softness and gullibility of the outer world the means of the enjoyment he desiderates. To this end he arrays himself and goes forth. The world of a garrison town is all before him whence to choose; and, although his cordial detestation is a "dry walk," he trusts to luck and impudence to moisten it ere it is over. This is the gentleman we see listlessly promenading the parks, or sauntering aimlessly along the streets—"counting the lamp-posts," as it is called in barrack-room phraseology. If he is a lady-killer, it is odds that he figuratively knocks down and bags some silly servant girl, who has an eye for colour and her month's wages in her pocket; although in the empty state of his pocket he finds a delicacy in initiating the acquaintance without being able to proffer the ice-breaking refreshment. This is the style of gentleman who sometimes got into trouble about alleged Fenianism; he would drink with the devil, let alone a head-centre, if there was nothing to pay and "lashings of it," and would, with all the alacrity in the world, tackle either or both next day at the word of command. The cravings of drouth before now have tempted such a hero to enter a public-house, call for beer, and bolt it incontinently, without being in a position to pay for the same; and he has been known, when reduced to

D

frenzy, and unrestrained by the proper pride of a British dragoon, to dip unsolicited his martial beak into other men's pots. And if his walk has been utterly barren and literally "dry," it is still a religious tenet with him to return at night to the barrack-room with simulated roll in his gait and a thickness in his speech, and to boast of "the pyke"—that is, the civilian simpleton—at whose charges he has got a skinful. This simulated intoxication is known in every barrack-room in Britain under the appellation of "slamming."

AT THE CHRISTMAS CATTLE MARKET.

AT THE CHRISTMAS CATTLE MARKET.

THE streets of London are perhaps never quieter than in the small hours of the night between Sunday and Monday. The public-houses close at eleven o'clock on Sunday night ; there are no homeward-bounders abroad returning in a more or less roystering fashion from the theatres, and the Sabbath night is especially an in-doors one with most respectable people.

When, on one December Monday morning about two o'clock, I sallied out on my way to the region of Copenhagen Fields, the streets were in a state of perfect quietude. The street-cleaner had not yet commenced his avocations, and the only living things I encountered were an occasional policeman, who, in accordance with the assumption current in "the force," that every one out-of-doors in the small hours is *primâ facie* a rogue, looked me hard in the face as I passed him ; here and there a bundle of dirty rags, presumably containing a human being, huddled up in some sheltered corner ; and now and then a roving cat. But as I passed King's Cross, and walked briskly up the Caledonian Road, there came wafted to me on the night-wind a faint hoarse roar, which, as I came nearer, I was gradually able to analyse, and found it to consist in about equal proportions of the

lowing of cattle, the shouts of men, and the sharp
bark of dogs. Its full volume burst upon me as I
topped the hill, and in a few minutes more I was close
to the great cattle market. Every road was thronged
with an apparently inextricable confusion of cattle,
all converging from every point of the compass into
the enclosure of the market-ground. Ponderous foot-
sore brutes, laden with fat, are mixed up with the
wild, active Highlanders, showing picturesquely
through the obscurity, with their shaggy coats and
great spreading horns ; uncountable droves of sheep
are blended with random bullocks, seemingly out on
their own account. The lairs surrounding the market in every direction are being disgorged into it, a
process which commences immediately upon the
stroke of twelve, and goes on without intermission up
till close upon daybreak.

Inside the enclosure of the market there is, to the
inexperienced eye, confusion worse confounded. Men
are shouting, yelling, and using their sticks as freely
as their voices, without the object being exactly apparent ; bullocks are here, there, and everywhere, involved in a chaos out of which it seems impossible to
evolve a system of order. Nevertheless, the system
is going on briskly. Beast after beast is caught by a
noose round the throat, and immediately made fast
to the series of strong pales which run right athwart
the market. Every man knows his work, and contrives to perform it with a dexterity and speed utterly
incomprehensible to the uninitiated. Even now, at
3 A.M., rows upon rows of cattle are already in
position and tied up, wedged together as closely as
herrings in a barrel. But these are merely cases in

the wild desert of confusion. Fresh droves are constantly arriving, heralded with much shouting and bawling, and as cattle are driven, or run frantically this way and that way, a position in the midst of the hubbub is a very trying one to the man of weak nerves ; for, turn which way you will, you seem always in the way, and extremely likely to be cleared out of it by a sudden rush. The drovers, however, are quite in their element, and avail themselves with magic adroitness of their thorough knowledge of bovine idiosyncracies. They pilot their charges into port with really wonderful celerity, and a system of mutual co-operation, taking the form of an opportunely administered blow, or a shout just in the nick of time, helps on matters greatly.

Even at this early hour the White Horse is in full swing, and doing a roaring trade. The floor of the bar is bedded with straw. In common with all the public-houses about the market, it has two counters —one being the ordinary public-house zinc-topped counter, the other a long wooden bar, over which coffee, tea, and the most substantial of eatables are being vended with great briskness. It is pleasant to observe that the latter department is the one by far the more extensively patronised. Slices of bread and butter of astounding thickness, great cups of scalding tea and coffee, are being served with promptitude and dexterity, and are disappearing with even greater alacrity. The huge rounds of beef in the background are getting "small by degrees and beautifully less" before the demands of the sharp-set applicants for frequent plates.

The customers about this hour consist almost

entirely of drovers who have just rushed in for a
snack in the midst of their labours, and one has a
capital opportunity of studying what manner of
man the drover is. A strong family likeness is apparent at first sight. Of course there is the tall
drover, and, again, there is the short drover, just as
we see similar differences in other varieties of the
human family ; but the type is the same, allowing for
variations of size. He is as lean as a hurdle—a fat
drover would be a *lusus naturæ.* His head is of a
peculiar pear shape ; his hair is straight, lank, and so
closely clipped as to suggest the " county crop," and
he makes all snug aloft with a round cap, something
of the skull-cap order, into which his head gets well
home. A neckcloth—or perhaps a fogle is the more
appropriate word—encircles his long crane neck with
many a fold ; and then we come to his coat, a most
peculiar structure. It is not a surtout, not an Oxford,
not a Newmarket, but a compound of all three, with
a dash of the gamekeeper's shooting-coat thrown in.
Its material is generally moleskin which has once been
white ; its waist is absurdly long, and the skirts are
both full and long, yet lapping closely to his lean
flanks. His legs are of the spindle pattern, tightly
encased in corduroys, which display to the fullest advantage his bony knee-joints, and being short, show
the ankle-jack in its full development. The gait of
the drover is a thing by itself. He never took a stride
in his life. He keeps his legs well under him, with
his knees always slightly bent, and covers the ground
with a short, brisk, tripping, springhalty action, exclusively the characteristic of him and no other man.
Whoever saw a drover without a stick—a long, supple

ash plant of tried and proven toughness ?   Or without
a dog ?   And the drover's dog merits a word for himself.   I don't think he can be classed under any breed
in particular, unless, indeed, we style him a pure-bred
mongrel.   If his pedigree is obscure, his sagacity is
unquestionable.   He does everything but speak, and
apparently *ex proprio motu*, for he wants no prompt-
ing to his work, always turning up just at the right
spot, and sticking to a wayward bullock with the
tenacity of a leech.   He is not of a gambolling or
frisky disposition.   He is far too matter-of-fact for
such gratuitous physical exertions ; and when he has a
moment of breathing-time, he sits deliberately down
on his hams and looks up in his master's face, as if to
ask whether his opinion of the arrangements his
helper has made is a favourable one.   I have not the
slightest doubt in my own mind that the drover's dog
understands the English language, at least as spoken
by drovers ; some of them perhaps the Dutch as well,
of which in the foreign cattle department a good deal
is spoken here.   He takes a mute, but deeply interested, part in every conversation his master enters
into, looking wisely into the face of each speaker in
turn, as if he were profoundly cogitating the sentiments uttered.

Four o'clock rings out from the clock tower, and the
confusion still seems as chaotic as ever, and the arteries
as much thronged.   The drovers are beginning to get
excited, and rush about hither and thither, shouting
wildly, and, sooth to say, swearing vehemently as
well.   It is about this time that we find them in too
many cases losing sight of the dictates of humanity,
and making vicious prods at the nostrils and eyes of

refractory stubborn animals, or using the tail as a sort
of screw-purchase to direct the motions of the body
to which it forms an appendix. Yet less wanton
cruelty is noticeable than preconceived ideas might
have led one to expect. It is when the drover is
thwarted and delayed by stubbornness or stupidity
that he gets vicious, and even then in most instances
there seems more semblance than reality of cruelty in
his rough-mouthed, and certainly too ready-handed
exertions to get over his work.

Five o'clock, and things are beginning to get
more shipshape, although the fresh arrivals are still
very frequent. We can now take a stroll up the
alleys between the closely-packed rows of cattle
without running an imminent risk of being incontinently trampled under hoofs in a stampede. It
is hardly worth while though, for all we can see
is the great white faces of the Herefords staring
at us out of the darkness, and here and there a pair
of branching horns, a knowledge of whose propinquity
we are apt to acquire, if we are not all the more careful, through the medium of another faculty besides
that of sight.

Every now and then we stumble across a man
moving slowly along, and handling the cattle as
he goes, trying to make the sense of touch super-
sede that of sight. We set him down—perhaps
wrongly—as a butcher who has got up very early in
the morning in order to take time by the forelock—a
decidedly unsatisfactory attempt to all appearance in
this instance. The drovers are clearly not partial to
him; they answer his questions curtly and evasively, and
evidently regard him as something of an interloper.

By and by another style of men appear on the scene, and they are received very differently. Sturdy bucolic parties these are, with comfortable paunches most of them, and low-crowned, broad-brimmed hats, and gaiters. They all stand on very short legs in proportion to their stature, and speak with a full-mouthed breadth of dialect, which at once proclaims them not to be Londoners. They are the owners of stock, men who have a liking for seeing all things right with their own proper eyes, rather than trust implicitly to the arrangements of the salesman; and they are making a preliminary inspection on their own account, now and then making a suggestion to the drover in charge, who displays plenty of alacrity in carrying their wishes into effect.

About half-past six there comes a lull in the bustle. The arrangement of the great majority of the stock has been satisfactorily completed, and most of the people employ the interval before daylight in snatching a hurried breakfast. The coffee-room of the White Horse is seething full. The butchers, and the dealers, and salesmen, by this time begin to put in an appearance, and everybody seems to know everybody. A curious feature is the hail-fellow-well-met style of pure democracy which exists. A drover and a swell young butcher are quietly confabulating in a corner. A knot of Dutch dealers are smoking long cigars and talking their own language over their coffee with very un-Dutchmanlike volubility. A stout farmer and a knowing-looking salesman are comparing notes in front of the fire. Everybody connected with the market, except the butchers, seems to consider it Hoyle to wear drab greatcoats

of jean, moleskin, or mackintosh. The drab greatcoat
is apparently the badge of the cattle trade. The
butchers don't affect it, but they fly a distinguishing
pennant of their own. We see them rattling up to the
White Horse in hansom cabs, and the moment they
are in the coffee-room they pull out a neatly-folded
blue apron, and gravely tie it round their waist. The
swell butcher—purveyor, as he chooses to call himself—displays the apron as religiously as the Whitechapel or New Cut cag-dealer, who seems to have
washed his face in suet, just as he is given to rubbing
bad meat with fat to improve its appearance.

Gradually, as daylight peers dimly in through the
windows, the bustle in the tavern decreases. The
great business of the day, buying and selling, to
which what we have already seen is but the preliminary, is commencing, and everybody makes for the
market enclosure. Here we now find everything in
apple-pie order. Men are shaking down straw underneath the cattle, not for them to rest on, for they are
not allowed to lie down, but to show them off to
better advantage. Close by the entrance is a row of
splendid Herefords, gigantic brutes, in tip-top condition, with white face and vast spreading horns. Farther on we come on a batch of picked Devons, with
their beautiful deer-like heads, and plump, even,
juicy carcases. They seem to carry more flesh than
the Herefords, because they are smaller in the bone.
Here is a row of wild and shaggy little Scotch
Highlanders, all horns and hair. At first sight they
look like a cross between a Scotch terrier and a
bison. Their native heather never made them so
fat; these layers of prime beef owe their existence

to the rich pasture-lands of Norfolk, upon which the
shaggy Scots, purchased lean at some Scotch tryst,
are put to fatten, and then finished off with turnips
and oilcake. A step farther, and we are amongst the
Scotch polls and crosses, sent up annually to this
market by the great Aberdeenshire and Morayshire
feeders. Here is a tier of great oxen, each one in
primer condition than the other, with the "M'C."
branded on the hip, the sign-manual of the far-famed
Tillyfour. He might have sent the "whole fleet" to
the cattle show; the mighty son of Black Prince was
merely the pick of the lot. All round them are the
consignments of Mr M'Combie's northern compeers,
and Messrs Dickson and Giblett, the salesmen the
north countrymen specially affect, can well afford to
put on an affectation of indifference to purchasers,
for they will get their own price from half-a-dozen
offerers at once. Around them are concentrated the
principal buyers of prime meat, who don't chaffer
about shillings so long as they get the quality they
want.

There is a special knot of admirers around six
great beasts which stand loose close by the clock
tower. They are the top of the market. Four of
them are polls, one a cross, and one a shorthorn, and
they are the giants of their kind. An Aberdeenshire
breeder sends them up, and the beast with which he
carried off the prize in the Agricultural Hall was not
a whit superior in condition or size to these splendid
cattle. Going farther, we fall on long rows of
Irish and foreign cattle — some very large and in
really capital condition; others miserable scarecrows
of leanness, destined for summary conversion into

sausage-meat in the purlieus of Bethnal Green and Whitechapel. A noticeable thing is that here and there, in the very midst of the primest cattle, we find tied up to the end of a row a miserable skeleton of an old cow—a wretch seemingly in an advanced state of atrophy. Whether she comes there by chance, or whether she is placed purposely as a foil to the splendid condition of her neighbours, we have no means of ascertaining; but that the salesmen know a trick or two is obvious, from the great care always taken to put the best animal of a lot on the outside, where his broadside is exposed.

The great Christmas cattle market, the muster-roll of which shows over 8000 cattle and 20,000 sheep, is between eight and ten o'clock at its height. The salesmen are in their glory, and are evidently having "a good time." By twelve all the best animals will have found buyers—indeed, by ten more than half of them are sold; and in another week there will not be a single head of all this vast number of fat cattle alive. In a fortnight's time the voracious maw of London will have left nothing but the bare bones. All this show is but a Christmas week's provender for the mighty Babylon.

SOLDIERS' WIVES.

SOLDIERS' WIVES.*

IN our regimental library I am unable to find any information as to whether the wives of Roman soldiers dwelt in the Prætorium, the Castrum, or the Vallum. Nor have I been more successful in gathering any details as to the early history of the wife of the British soldier—when she first became a recognised institution in the service, and what was the nature of the first privileges accorded to her. I requested a friend in London to make some inquiry on the subject at headquarters, but the result was by no means encouraging. He went first to the War Office, whence they sent him to the Horse Guards. But the Horse Guards "did not know,—you know," and so he came empty away. So I leave to some one else, with better opportunities, the task of dealing with the historical part of the subject, and with no affectation of regret because of the narrowing of my bounds, I will confine myself to narrating what

* The article under this heading is one of a series contributed to *St Paul's Magazine* under the signature of "A Private Dragoon." The condition of the soldier's wife has been considerably improved during Mr Cardwell's tenure of office. A recent order enacts the beneficent provision that threepence a day may be deducted from the soldier's pay for the maintenance of his wife, even if he has married "without leave."

33   C

has come under my own observation since I joined
Her-Majesty's Service, with respect to the condition,
habits, morality, and manner of life generally of the
private soldier's wife.

It was before I became an unit in the muster-roll
of Britain's defenders, that the women of the regiment
who were married with leave—technically, "on the
strength"—lived, without exception, in the barrack-
room among the men. There were commonly a
married couple in each room. To them, through
long consuetude, was assigned the corner farthest
from the door. No matter what their number in
family might be, they were allowed but two single
bedsteads, and two men's room. No privacy of any
kind was afforded them, save what they could contrive for themselves; and the married soldier was
wont to rig up around his matrimonial bower an environment of canvas screening, something over six
feet high, and enclosing a very little domain of floor-
space in addition to that occupied by the two beds,
placed together. In most regiments the "woman of
the room" cooked for the room at the fireplace
therein, in return for which office it was customary
for a "mess" to be cut off for her out of the men's
rations; for in the days of which I am speaking
married couples were entitled to no rations—this
arrangement is one of the beneficent outcomes of the
commissariat system. The married man was put out
of mess, and he had wherewithal to maintain himself
and his family nothing save his bare pay, in addition
to anything that the wife might earn.

The very idea of a married couple living and sleeping
in a common room with a dozen or more of single men,

partitioned off but by a flimsy curtain, is outrageously
repulsive to our sense of decency. One may well be
struck with wonderment that the arrangement should
have been left uninterfered with so long. When the
soldier got married in those times he strained every
effort, it is true, gradually to acclimatise his wife to
the barrack-room, fresh as she was, in many cases,
from a quiet country cottage, or from service in a
decent family. He was wont to take lodgings outside for the first week of the married life, so that at
least the earliest quarter of the honeymoon should be
invested with some of the sacred privacy of which
there was to be so little afterwards. But men have
told me how they have seen a pure girl brought
straight from the church to the barrack-room corner,
and the tremor of mortal shame that overwhelmed
her. It wore off, as most things of the kind mercifully do wear off, under exposure to the chafe of
custom and necessity; but the bride's blushes for
herself fell to be renewed at an after period on the
tanned cheek of the mother.

Children were not, indeed, born in the corner; the
woman, when her time was near at hand, was removed
to lodgings outside, where, at her husband's expense,
she tarried till her recovery; but in the corner daughters
grew from childhood to girlhood, with but the screen
between them and the men outside. When a daughter
fell out of place, all the home she had to come to was
the corner; and it was noways uncommon for grown
women to sleep therein, on the top of the chest,
alongside the bed of their parents. When the family
was large, living, or at all events sleeping, in the corner was little better than pigging, strictly limited as

the authorised sleeping accommodation was to the
two narrow regulation bedsteads. The woman used
to dispose of her boys in the vacant beds of soldiers
who were on duty ; but in the case of girls there was
nothing for it but close packing behind the screen.

Bad as all this was—disgusting in theory, and repulsive, in many respects, in practice—there were in it,
strange as it may seem, some compensatory elements
of good. Although the woman had to reconcile herself, with what contentment she might, to a life that
perpetually violated the instincts of womanhood, she
simply became blunted, not degraded. In proportion
as she lived in public, she felt herself amenable to
public opinion as represented by the little world of
her room ; and lowly as her sphere was, and rough as
too often became her manners and speech, underneath the skin-deep blemishes there lay self-respect
and discretion. She would take her share of a gallon
of porter at the common table, but she durst not get
drunk, conscious as she was of the critics of her conduct around her. And she made the barrack-room
more of a home—of a family circle—than it is to-day.
The men of her room looked upon her in some such
light as they would upon a sister keeping house for
them. On a change of quarters they always struggled
hard to keep their coterie together, with the same
woman for its presiding genius. She humanised the
barrack-room with the sacred influence of her true if
somewhat rough womanhood. There was far less
profanity among the men then than there is now ;
and that obscenity of habitual expression which must
startle and shock any visitor to the barrack-room of
to-day, was unknown then, quelled wholly by the

woman within hearing. Ruffians there were in the
service then as there are now, and an outbreak of
foul language sometimes came from the lips of one
of them. But he was sternly put down and silenced ;
if a hint from an old soldier, and the finger pointed
toward the screen did not suffice, a straight right-
hander formed a ready and very convincing argument.

The woman was a kindly, motherly soul to the
forlorn "cruitie," and would cheer him up with
homely words of encouragement as he sat on his bed-
iron mopingly thinking of home. She was always
obliging if you entreated her civilly, whether to sew
on a button or lend a shilling. If she was anything
of a scholar, to her fell the office of letter-writer-
general for the fellows whose penmanship had been
neglected in early days, and thus she became the
repository of not a few confidences, which she scorned
to violate. Sometimes, as an especial favour, she
would allow a man to bring his sweetheart on a Sunday afternoon to a modest tea within the screen in
the corner; and if friends came from a distance to
see one of "her men," the married woman was
always ready to do her best for the credit's sake of
the hospitality of her room. There can be little doubt
that fewer scandals were current in those days about
married women than there are now, and I question
much whether, accepting the roughness of the husk
as a necessary outcome of their situation, the women
who dwelt in the corners were not more genuine at
the core than are the ladies who now inhabit the
married quarters.

Besides the evils I have alluded to, there was
another connected with the position of the former

that must not be forgotten. Soldiers are very fond of children, but are apt to look upon them in the light rather of monkeys than of creatures with souls in their little bodies. So the imps grew up tutored in all manner of tricks—developing a weird precocity in tossing off a basinful of porter and smoking the blackest of pipes, and using not the most choice language. Mostly they went either into the band of the regiment, or into one of the military schools; and thus, under the old long-service regime, the country had an hereditary soldiery, not a few of whom, born at the foot of the regimental ladder, have climbed up it no inconsiderable distance.

In the days I now speak of, there were few railways save some of the great trunk lines. When a regiment went on the line of march, the women rode on the accompanying baggage-waggons, with their brats stowed away in odd corners among the other miscellaneous goods and chattels, and went to their husband's billet, if the people were willing to admit them—as, to their credit, they mostly were. When they were not, the husband had to find lodgings for his wife somewhere else; and when the funds were low, it was customary for women to be smuggled into the hay-loft above the troop-horses, and sometimes even to bivouac on the lee-side of a hedge. To some extent the railways entailed an additional charge on the married soldier's slender purse. He had always had to pay for his baggage; for the chest or two, the feather bed,—if the couple had got that length in prosperity,—and the few feminine belongings which the wife could call her own; but now the husband had to pay for the warrant under which his wife and

family were conveyed by rail. Within the last ten
years, however, "baggage-funds" have been formed
in most regiments, the proceeds of which go far to
meet the travelling charges of the women and children
of the regiment. In the days I refer to, if women had
to live outside the barracks because of want of room
inside, there was no allowance in the shape of lodging
money. The first grant of this was made, I think, in
1852, and consisted of one penny a day, paid quarterly.
It was gradually increased, till now I believe the
allowance is fourpence per day.

This may be taken as a rough epitome of the condition of the soldier's wife up till the end of 1848, or
the beginning of 1849. About that period, I think,
through some troubles in the financial world, an exceptional number of better-class men joined the service, and struck with the indecency of the arrangement
then in force, not a few sent in anonymous complaints
to the Horse Guards ; others, through the press,
stimulated public opinion to demand a change, and
the authorities sluggishly complied. The reform
was not carried through with any great promptitude,
for I have heard of women living in the barrack-rooms
after the Crimean war. But the change was made in
the regiment to which I belonged in the year 1849. It
was no great change for the better. Into one attic in
Christchurch Barracks seven families were huddled
pell-mell. No more arrangements for privacy were
made than had existed in the common barrack-rooms.
Each separate *ménage* was curtained off by what may
be styled private enterprise. There was but one fireplace in the room, and the women squabbled vehemently over their turns for cooking, and were forced

to have recourse to the fires in the men's barrack-
rooms.

The moral and social tone was visibly deteriorated
under this arrangement below that which had charac-
terised the common barrack-room. The women, con-
gregated as they were, and with no check upon them,
were too prone to club for gin, and conviviality was
chequered with quarrels, into which the husbands
were not unfrequently drawn. There was a perceptible
growth of coarseness of tone among both the women
and the men, that became actual grossness; and I
question if a young woman, with some of Nature's
modesty clinging to her, did not have it more violently
outraged in this congeries of married couples than
would have been the case in the old corner-of-the-
barrack-room arrangement. Of this at least I am
certain, that with ominous rapidity she learned to talk,
and would submit to be jeered, on subjects which were
ignored under the old system.

The over-crowding, also, which was all but universal,
was physically injurious to both adults and children.
The latter did not count in allocating quarters. I have
known ten families in one long room in Weedon Barracks. Eight families in a hut in the North Camp at
Aldershot was nothing uncommon. But a better *régime*
is now rapidly obtaining. There are few barracks
now which do not contain married quarters; where
each couple have a room to themselves. I know not
whether the inception of this new system was due to
our gracious Queen, but the rapidity with which
married quarters have become all but universal is,
certainly owing in the main to her womanly sympathy
with her sex.

Still, however, these married quarters in many cases do not afford sufficient accommodation, and the surplusage have to fall back on the old system. The summer before last, in Aldershot,* more than one troop-room was occupied by four families, and as I write, I doubt not that about a third of the married strength of the home forces are still unaccommodated with separate rooms. In civilian estimation a single room for a man and wife and their family,—day-room and bed-room in one,—seems no great boon ; but the soldier and his wife have been so little used to mercies of any kind, that they are thankful for very small ones. Yet a second room, if not for the married private, at least for the non-commissioned officer of the higher grade, might with advantage be conceded. A squadron sergeant-major is a non-commissioned aristocrat ; his position in the military cosmos being roughly analogous to that of the managing foreman of a factory in the civilian world. But how would the latter relish having to pay his hands, the head of the concern sitting with him at the pay-table, while his recently-confined wife lay in bed in the same room, sequestered only by a curtain ? †

The soldier does not very often go to his own home for a wife. He forgets the sweetheart of his pre-soldiering days, and finds another where he may chance to be quartered. Most soldiers' wives have been servant girls, with whom the militaire has picked acquaintance casually in his evening strolls. But

* This was written in 1867.
† This is no fancy picture. I have signed accounts in the Royal Barracks in Dublin, when my troop sergeant-major's domestic ménage was in the condition described.

there are many exceptions, and some of these of rather
a sensational kind.   I once knew a soldier's wife who
had been a clergyman's daughter, another who had
been a vocalist at a leading music-hall, and a third
who had been the widow of a captain in the navy.
Since the relaxation in the rigour exercised in regard
to marriages without leave—to which I shall presently
have occasion to advert—soldiers have more and more
taken to marrying prostitutes.   Repulsive as such a
connection is, fairness demands the admission that
these women, with very few exceptions, turn out well-
conducted wives.   I suppose they are so weary of their
previous life, that to be a wife at all, no matter how
humble the sphere, is a coveted haven of refuge too
deeply appreciated to be lightly forfeited.   At all
events, the fact is as I state.

So prone are soldiers to take their wives from among
the daughters of the land in which they may be stationed, that an experienced hand can map out by the
different strata, so to speak, of married womanhood in
a regiment, the track of its journeyings from district to
district.   Let me give an example from my own regiment, as I knew it.   The mothers of the corps are south
of England women—Christchurch and Brighton ex-
tracts, decently inclined, self-respecting, rather masculine dames, who have followed the kettle-drums many
a year, and got tanned and travel-worn, but honest,
cleanly, blunt of speech, and fairly pure of heart.
Then comes a layer of canny Scotch lassies, picked
up during a tour in the north country, clannish to
the last degree, grasping, and greedy most of them ;
" wearing the breeches" as regards their " gudemen,"
but good wives, nevertheless, and excellent mothers ;

fond of a "drappie," when somebody else pays for it, mostly with a nest-egg in the regimental savings-bank, and willing to do a little bit of usury on the quiet, very unpopular with the other women, horribly quarrelsome, and scrupulously clean. Then comes a miscellaneous infusion of the Irish element, resulting from the corps having been stationed for several years in various parts of the sister isle. Irish women, with few exceptions, do not make good soldiers' wives. They are too ready to accommodate themselves to circumstances, instead of striving to make circumstances bend to them; thus in the unfavourable phase of life in which they find themselves through marrying a soldier, they are prone to go with the swim, to become careless and slatternly, to say, "sufficient for the day is the evil thereof," and to be heedless if to-morrow's pot portends emptiness so long as to-day's "boils fat."

When the soldier falls a prey to matrimonial long-ings, he obtains an interview with his colonel in the orderly-room, and formally asks permission to get married. If he has any length of service and a good character, permission is grudgingly given him, subject to the occurrence of a vacancy in his squadron or company. If he is a sensible man he waits for this, and then his wife is at once "taken on the strength," and is entitled to her share of the privileges that are going. A certain number of men, commonly the inmates of one room, are assigned her to "do for." She washes the weekly budget of very dirty clothes, and in most cavalry regiments she still has the task of keeping the room clean. She scrubs it over daily, keeps the tables and forms in a snow-white state, washes the crockery-ware after each meal, and generally has to satisfy the captain as to the cleanliness of the apartment. In other cavalry regiments the men perform these functions in rotation, and the woman has merely the washing to do. In either case each of her men pay her a penny a day. The charge in infantry regiments is but a halfpenny, and there the men are invariably their own housemaids. In some regiments of the latter branch of the service, the married women are prohibited altogether from entering the barrack-rooms.

Those women who do not have a certain number of men assigned them, look after an officer a piece, at the remuneration of a shilling a day; but this is an employment which falls chiefly to the wives of non-commissioned officers. The husband, for his part, does his best to contribute to the exchequer. Sometimes he is detailed as an officer's servant, an office which brings him in 10s. or 15s. per month, besides perquisites ; or if he is not lucky enough for this, he may undertake the care of a sergeant's horse, for which he gets 10s. per month. In all, I reckon the weekly income of a couple in a cavalry regiment, when the husband is earning his 10s. per month in addition to his pay, and the wife is making a shilling a day, to amount to about a guinea a week *—no bad income, when it is remembered that no rent comes out of it, and that the husband has hardly any clothing to pay for. An additional privilege is the right to draw one ration of three-quarters of a pound of meat and one pound of bread for 4½d.,

* This refers to a period anterior to the 2d. per diem addition to the soldier's pay

about one-half the price retail in the open market. Till lately, two rations were allowed to be drawn, but this has been stopped for reasons of economy. I know of no deduction from the above estimate, save barrack damages, and the recently-imposed halfpenny per day for bedding, if its exaction be persisted in.

The soldier's wife is commonly an utter heathen as regards religion, unless she is a Roman Catholic, and then she is no less a heathen for the dash of superstition. She cannot go to the garrison church in the forenoon because of her barrack-room and domestic duties, and it is very seldom she ever goes to church at all. With the exception of one or two stations, to the chaplains of which all honour is due, she seldom or never receives a clerical visit. The chaplain mostly seems to consider that when he does his pulpit work he earns his pay, and I suppose the civilian minister shuns the barracks lest he should be thought to be poaching on the chaplain's domain. I might be per-mitted to suggest to well-intentioned ladies in towns where there are barracks, what an excellent field lies fallow in the married quarters for judicious cultiva-tion. One of the greatest evils of a married woman's lot in the army is her isolation from humanising civilian influences. So precarious is her term of resi-dence anywhere, that she soon ceases any effort to cultivate acquaintance outside the barrack-gate; and if she would not be utterly companionless, she must fall back upon her sisters of the regiment for society. She is none the better for the defiant pariah-feeling that this concentration is apt to engender.[*]

[*] There is considerable alteration for the better in the above respects since these lines were written.

Hitherto I have been writing of soldiers' wives who have become so in a strictly constitutional and regimental manner. But for one soldier who marries "with leave," at least half a dozen marry without leave. Sometimes a man applies for leave, which is either refused or postponed. In the majority of cases, circumstances render the formality of asking leave a needless farce, and he marries without troubling to go through it. Rules affecting men married without leave vary according to the dispositions— severe or lenient—of commanding officers. In my early soldiering days, I knew a man who had been married for twenty years, a man with an excellent character, and holding non-commissioned rank, whose wife was never taken on the strength of the regiment at all, because the marriage had been without leave. In some regiments a probation, or rather a purgatory, of eight years had to be undergone before the offence of getting married without permission was condoned, and the wife admitted to privileges. Of late years, a more lenient policy has come into operation. A suitable applicant is permitted to marry at once, with the promise that his wife will be taken "on the strength" in rotation, and meanwhile a little work is assigned her to ease the hardship of her lot. Prior to this, it was usual for the soldier and his wife to be married twice over, the second marriage taking place when leave was granted, in order to meet the necessity of the registration of the marriage lines in the orderly-room, when the production of the record of the first marriage would have exposed the disobedience of orders, and led to a retractation of the permission. I remember a critical legitimacy question once arising out of a double marriage of this kind.

To get married without leave, even although it be accompanied by no other infraction of discipline, is a military crime coming under the head of disobedience of orders, and I have known a man severely punished for the offence. But most frequently marriage without leave is aggravated by the crime of concurrent absence, and the offender is punished nominally for the latter, but in reality for the other also. Thus, I have known a man get seven days' cells, involving the loss of his hair, for a couple of hours' absence in the morning for the purpose of getting married. It is not pleasant, it must be confessed, to meet your bride with not so much hair on your head as would supply a locket. Not unfrequently, in the stern wrath of the commanding officer, the woman's name "is put on the gate," *i.e.*, she is prohibited from entering the barracks. Her plight is a very sad one. She has left her place or her father's home, and it is with her "nulla vestigia retrorsum." She lingers wistfully about the barrack gate, pitifully asking the men as they walk out what punishment her husband has got, and when it will be over. She gets a room somewhere near the barracks, and her husband half starves himself, that he may share his food with her, and his mates cut him the bigger mess when they know that it has to feed two mouths.

It is seldom that this self-deniant method of feeding a wife is interfered with. The only instance which occurs to me took place some years ago at Belfast, by order of Colonel Hobbs, of Jamaica mutiny notoriety, the harshest disciplinarian I have ever known. With but few exceptions, the man acts very loyally by the woman with whom he has rashly formed a union. Sometimes, it is true, things do go wrong. The woman gives up the hard battle in despair, and enters on a more wretched campaign still, with sure defeat as its inevitable ghastly close; or the husband rebels against the necessary self-denial, and shirks his responsibility. But much oftener the twain cling together with a piteous yet a proud devotion. The compassionate matrons who are on the strength give the woman a turn on washing days, or she picks up some employment about the officers' mess kitchen, or among the non-commissioned officers' wives.

A change of station is a heavy blow to the struggling couple. There is no "warrant" for the woman married without leave, and it is not often that her husband can compass the railway fare. I have known a woman foot it all the way from Aldershot to Edinburgh, marching day for day with her husband's troop, sometimes getting into his billet at night, but oftener located in the hay-loft. Long ere she crossed Kelso Bridge, her boots had given out; but her heart was tougher than her boots, and she triumphantly reached Jock's Lodge only a few hours behind her husband. Shorter journeys of this kind are common enough, not only with soldiers' wives, but with females who have no such tie with the men they follow.

A time sometimes comes, however, to the woman married without leave when her courage is of no avail—when the regiment is ordered on foreign service,—and she is left straining her eyes through bitter hopeless tears after the receding troopship. Now she is, indeed,

alone in the world. But she turns instinctively bar-
rackward—there is consolation, seemingly, in the
colour of the cloth. There is hardly a barrack of any
size in the kingdom where there are not, as hangers
on, some of these compulsory grass-widows, picking
a precarious livelihood by the merciful consideration
of soldiers' wives better circumstanced. Such an one,
as she wrestles single-handed with the world, is counting longingly the years and the months till her husband's term of service shall expire. It may be that
one day a letter arrives from a chum, or a discharged
soldier of her husband's regiment strolls into barracks
with the tidings that Bill or Joe is dead of cholera at
some unhealthy inland station, or that fever took him
off in some forced march through the jungle. But,
again, Bill or Joe is back himself, with his discharge
in his pocket and love in his heart, and the horizon
becomes very rosy to the poor barrack-drudge. But
such a case as I have pictured is rarer since the relaxation in the stringency of the rules, the details
of which are given above.

I would fain, for the credit of the cloth, correct a
prevalent impression that the soldier is an habitual
bigamist—that, as the saying goes, "he has a wife in
every town he lies in." His morality is blunt enough,
but he seldom perpetrates more than one marriage.
Indeed, were he so inclined, he would find that
luxury dashed by disagreeable consequences. The
woman once married to a soldier is not to be shaken
off by any such trifle as a change of station. She
will track him like a blood-hound, and one day the
inevitable message is sure to reach him from the gate
that he is "wanted" by his wife persistent, if unwel-

D

come.   The woman married to a soldier who wishes to evade his obligations has struck me as resembling that well-known institution, "the guard-room dog" —an animal of a resolute turn of mind—the more he is turned out the more he is determined to come in. You can't lose him; he won't starve; tin-kettles attached to his tail are of no avail; kicks, buffets, and scorn are alike unheeded by him, till at length, through sheer force of persistency, he makes good his position, and establishes his right to inhabit the guard-room, and to the reversion of the scraps.

IN A MILITARY PRISON.

IN A MILITARY PRISON.

" DRUNK on the line of march " is an offence regarded
in the army as a very heinous one, not to be punished
summarily, but to be dealt with by a court-martial.
Nor is this unreasonable, because troops on the march
are always supposed by a fiction to be in an enemy's
country, and therefore constantly on active duty and
in a condition fit for any service. Intoxication must
deteriorate this fitness, and therefore it is that the
crime is considered so serious, and punished with so
much severity.

The old " Strawboots " were on the road from Liverpool to Sheffield, and we were billeted for the night
at an outlandish village among the Derbyshire hills,
called Chapel-en-le-Frith. My billet happened to be
what soldiers call a first-rate one—that is, there was
unlimited beer gratis. Now, it is a characteristic of
the malt liquor of these parts both to be very heady
and to possess the property of keeping in the head
an unconscionable length of time. If, therefore, it is
mentioned that I was imbibing this treacherous fluid
with so much appreciation that I forgot to go to bed,
my condition in the morning when the trumpet
sounded " turn out " may be easily imagined. I could

53

just manage to keep outside my mare, but that was
all, and to add to my discomfiture, the old jade,
ordinarily the sedatest of the sedate, as became a
veteran quadruped who had weathered the Crimean
war, acted on this particular morning as if she too
had been on the spree, and was as frisky as a two-
year-old. I had barely reached the parade-ground
when the lynx-eyed lieutenant "spotted" me, and
in a twinkling the order, "Dismount that man;
he's infernally drunk!" rang in my ears. With some
difficulty I effected a satisfactory dismount, and in
doing so a bright thought, a last squeak for liberty,
occurred to me.

Be it known unto all men, that the soldier accused
of intoxication can demand the test of an ordeal.* He
may claim to be put through his "facings," and if he
can accomplish this satisfactorily, he can demand to
be adjudged sober, though he be palpably as drunk as
David's sow. Many is the cunning old militaire who
has escaped the guard-room by this appeal to the
solidity of his understandings; and with a beery confidence in my own, I demanded to be put to the test.
In half a minute I was standing on the pavement at
"attention," with a grim old sergeant in front of me,
and in another, at the word "three-quarters left about
turn," I had executed a tremendous header over my
sword scabbard into the gutter. This sealed my fate;
my belts were speedily stripped, and I found myself
between two mounted men, doomed to foot it the five-
and-twenty miles into Sheffield under a burning sun.

I was in a state of abject sobriety when I reached
this town of armour-plates and knife-handles, and

* This has been abolished for some years.

was ignominiously thrust into the guard-room to await orders from the colonel, who, with headquarters, was still in Ireland. In about a week came the order for a "regimental court-martial" to be holden on my unfortunate carcase. When I received the statutory twenty hours' warning of the same, I knew at once what was to befall me, for this species of court, being limited in its punitive powers to the infliction of forty-two days' imprisonment, after the manner of such restricted tribunals, makes a point of awarding its maximum, and a verdict of acquittal by a regimental court-martial is a thing utterly unheard of. So I went before the court with a calmness begotten of foreknowledge, and went back to the guard-room again to await the colonel's approving fiat. In due time it arrived, and one fine morning I was brought out into the barrack square before a full-dress parade of the two squadrons to hear the major read the " Proceedings of a regimental court-martial held on No. 420, Private Blank Blank," &c., at which, after a number of witnesses being solemnly sworn and examined, " the said No. 420, &c., was found guilty, and sentenced to imprisonment for a period of forty-two days. Approved and confirmed, (signed) Marmaduke Sabretache, colonel." Reconducted to the guard-room, I spent the night there (the twelfth I had passed sleeping in my cloak on the boards), and at two o'clock next day was formally handed over to the sergeant in charge of the provost cells.

I was a young soldier, and had never been in trouble before. Tobacco is rigidly prohibited in prison, a strict search being made for the contraband article on admission; and devoted to the weed as I

was—prepared even to chew rather than not enjoy
it at all—my chief care was how to smuggle in my
luxury successfully.   I had plenty of advice from old
hands—one telling me to secrete an ounce in the
lining of my jacket, another recommending the boot
as a receptacle, and a third pronouncing in favour of
the small of the back ; but I planted a modicum inside the leather of my overalls, and was successful in
evading discovery.

Handed over to the provost-sergeant, the first
thing that functionary did was to "feel" me all
over carefully, in order to discover illegal articles,
and then he bestowed his attention on my kit with
the same benign intention, confiscating my knife
and fork, but leaving me my spoon, remarking
with saturnine humour that the latter would suffice
for the fare I should get there.   My razor also
was confiscated, most probably to guard against
suicidal intentions, and half a dozen coppers and a
sheet or two of writing-paper shared its fate, the sergeant grimly observing that I should have no occasion
for these commodities while under his care.   Then I
passed into the hands of a gentleman who, I afterwards came to know, combined the offices of cook and
that of professor of haircutting, of his dexterity in
which latter he at once proceeded to afford me convincing demonstration by denuding me in a twinkling
of hair, whiskers, and moustache, as close to the skin
as scissors could well go, leaving my head about as
bare as a turnip.

This operation performed, I was conducted to my
cell, and left to commune with my own thoughts,
and to make acquaintance with the extremely limited

area in which so much of the next forty-two days
was to be passed. It measured some eight feet
by six, lighted by a little window close to the
ceiling; the floor was of asphalte, and the furni-
ture consisted of a stool and an apology for a bed-
stead, in the shape of a couple of planks raised about
three inches from the floor, with a square wooden box
at the top, about four inches higher, by way of pillow.
Here I remained till eight o'clock, when my door was
unlocked, and I was called down to receive my cloak
and a basin of water, after which I was locked up again
for the night. No mattress or bedding was granted
me; indeed, they are withheld for the first seven
nights altogether, and are only accorded every alter-
nate night during the remainder of the term, with the
intent, I suppose, of making these luxuries the more
appreciated when they are allowed. But as during
my prior imprisonment in the guard-room I had got
used to sleeping on the planks, I did not feel the
deprivation very acutely.

Next morning I was called at six, and had an hour's
indoor work with my fellow-prisoners in cleaning our
cells and the stairs and corridors of the prison, under
the supervision of an orderly. At seven we were sum-
moned into the yard for an hour's shot-drill; and as
this agreeable pastime is probably new to the reader,
as it then was to me, a short explanation may not be
out of place. Suppose four blocks of wood, each
about four inches high, to be placed at the corners of
a square, each face of which is about three yards long.
On each block stands a 32-pound shot, and at the word
of command each of four prisoners stations himself in
front of a block in a line with the one behind him. At

the word "Lift," each man lifts his own shot, faces right-about, takes three paces, and deposits his shot on the block which was behind him as he faced his own. He returns empty-handed to find another shot on his own block, placed there by the man occupying the other face of the square. And so the work goes drearily on, the shot making the circuit of the square, and each man working in his own ground, making one journey shot-laden, and returning empty-handed. The constant stooping and lifting, which must be done with a straight leg, and without allowing the shot to touch the body, makes this very fatiguing work, and I can cheerfully recommend it to the notice of any gentleman who is troubled with wrinkles in the region of the spinal vertebræ. An hour at it we found an excellent appetiser for breakfast, which consisted of a basin of oatmeal porridge and half a pint of milk, with an hour to eat it in, and for rumination.

From nine till ten, kit-drill—*i.e.*, marching in quick time round the prison-yard in full dress, and with packed valises, weighing about a hundredweight, strapped on the back. From eleven till twelve another hour's shot-drill, and from twelve till one "fatigue" duty, in the shape of grass-picking, sweeping, or some kindred employment about the barracks, under the guardianship of the provost-sergeant. Dinner at one, consisting of three pounds of boiled potatoes—as sure as I'm *not* an Irishman—and half a pint of milk, with the customary hour's rest. From two till four kit-drill again, from four till five shot-drill, from five till six more "fatigue," and then supper, consisting of half a pound of bread and half a pint of milk ; locked up till eight, when we received our cloaks and cold water, and then the key was turned on us for the night.

One day may suffice as a true sample of all the others, save the Sundays, on which days we were marched into the barrack church; after service, had an hour's exercise, and enjoyed the sweets of solitary confinement for the remainder of the day. There was no alteration in the simple diet; and before my time was up I had almost forgotten the taste of butcher's meat. The first morning, when I received my mess of porridge, I had thought the contriver of the prison diet was a Scot; at dinner-time the potatoes imbued me with the idea that he was an Irishman; but when night and the bread came, I was bewildered altogether as to his nationality, and had to come to the conclusion that the scale had been organised by a committee which had made an elaborate effort to accommodate the taste in one meal or other of a prisoner belonging to each of the three countries, and I almost expected to see a leek served out for luncheon as a compliment to the Welsh contingent. Nevertheless, meagre as the fare was, I don't think we lost flesh—I know I weighed as much when I came out as when I went in; but the weakened stomach rebelled vehemently against a pint of beer and a beefsteak, charitably administered to me by a friendly neighbour on the afternoon of my liberation.

It must be noticed, in conclusion, that I served my term in a "garrison provost," and not in one of the large military gaols, such as Weedon, Chatham, or Aldershot, where the treatment is more strict, the diet rather more generous, and the periods of imprisonment much longer.

GERMAN WAR-PRAYERS.

GERMAN WAR-PRAYERS.

IN the multifarious ramifications of their military organisation, the Germans by no means neglect religion. Each army corps is partitioned into two divisions, and each division has its field-chaplain. In those corps in which there is a large admixture of the Catholic element, there is a cleric of that denomination to each division, as well as a Protestant chaplain. The former is known as a "Feldgeistliger," a word which in itself means nothing more distinctive than a "field ecclesiastic," while the Protestant chaplain has usually the title of "Feldpastor." Of the priest I can say but little. The pastors, for the most part, are young and energetic men. They may be divided into two classes : those who have at home no stated charges, and those who have temporarily left their charge for the duration of the war. The former generally are regularly posted to a division; the latter, equally recognised, but not perhaps quite so official, are chiefly to be found in the Lazarettes in the battlefield villages whither the wounded are borne to have their fresh wounds roughly seen to, and on the battlefield itself. Not that the regular divisional chaplains do not face the dangers of the battlefield

63

with devoted courage ; but their duties, in the nature
of their special avocation, lie more among the hale
and sound, who yet stand up before an enemy, than
with the poor fellows who have been stricken down.
Earnestness and devotion are the chief characteristics
of these pastors.   It struck me that their education
was not of a very high order—certainly not on a par
with that of the average regimental officer.

The Feldpastor wears an armlet of white and light
purple, to denote his calling; but indeed it is not easy
to mistake him for anything else than he is.   He has
his quarters with the Divisional General, and preaches
wherever it is convenient to get a congregation.   A
church is passed on the wayside, a regiment halts and
defiles into it, and the pastor mounts the steps of the
altar, and holds forth therefrom for half an hour.
There is a quiet meadow near a village, in which a
brigade is lying.   Looking over the hedge, you
may see in it a hollow square of helmeted men, with
the general and the pastor in the centre, the latter
speaking simple, fervent words to the fighting-men.
When, as in the siege of Paris, a division occupies a
certain district for a long time, you may chance—let
me say on a New-Year's night—on the village church
all ablaze with light.   The garrison have decorated
the gaunt old Norman arches with laurels and evergreens; they have cleared out the market-vendor's
stock of tallow-dips to illuminate the church wherewithal.   The band has been practising the glorious
" Nun danket alle Gott" for a week ; the vocalists of
the regiments have been combining to perfect themselves in part-singing.   The gorgeous trumpery of
Roman Catholic church-paraphernalia, unheeded as it

is, looks strangely out of place, and contrasts curiously with the simple Protestant forms.

The church is crowded with a denser congregation than ever its walls contained before. The Oberst sits down with the under-officer; the general gropes for half a chair between two stalwart *Kerle* of the line. Hymn-cards are distributed as at the Brighton volunteer service in the Pavilion on Easter Sunday. As the pastor enters and takes his way up the altar steps—he goes not to the pulpit—there bursts out a volume of vocal devotional harmony, which is so pent in the aisles and under the arches, that the sound seems almost to become a substance. Then the pastor delivers a prayer, and there is another hymn. He enunciates no text when he next begins to speak; he chops not a subject up into heads, as the grizzled major who listens to him would partition out his battalion into companies. There is no "thirteenthly and lastly" in his simple address. But he gets nearer the hearts of his hearers than if he assailed them with a battery of logic, with multitudinous texts for ammunition. For he speaks of the people at home, in the quiet corners of the Fatherland; he tells the soldier, in language that is of his profession, how the fear of the Lord is a better arm than the truest-shooting *Zündnadelgewehr;* how preparedness for death, and for what follows after death, is a part of his accoutrement that the good soldier must ever bear about with him.

Herr Pastor has other functions than to preach to the living. The day after a battle, his horse must be very tired before the stable-door is reached. The burial parties are excavating great pits all over the field, while others pick up the dead in the vicinity,

E

and bear them unto the brink of the common grave.
Herr Pastor cannot be ubiquitous. If he is not near
when the hole is full, the Feldwebel who commands
the party bares his head, and mutters, " In the name
of God, Amen," as he strews the first handful of
mould on the dead—it may be foes as well as friends.
If the pastor can reach the brink of the pit, it is his
to say the few words that mark the recognition of the
fact that those lying stark and grim below him are
not as the beasts that perish. The Germans have no
set funeral litany, and if they had there would be no
time for it here, " Earth to earth, ashes to ashes, dust
to dust, in sure and certain hope of the resurrection
to eternal life, 'durch unsern Herr Jesu Christe,'
Amen ;" words so familiar, yet never heard without
a new thrill.

They are slightly uncouth in several matters, these
Feldpastoren, and would not do for sundry metropolitan charges one wots of. They do not wear gloves,
nor are they addicted to scent in their pocket-hand-
kerchiefs. Their boots are too often like boats, and
when they are mounted, there is frequently visible an
interregnum of more or less dusky stocking between
the boot and the trouser. They slobber stertorously
in the consumption of soup, and cut their meat with
a square-elbowed energy of determination that might
make you think they had vanquished the Evil One,
and had him down there under their knife and fork.
But they are simple-hearted and valiant servants of
their Master. Who was it, in the bullet-storm that
swept the slope of Wörth, from facing which the stout
hearts of the fighting-men blenched and quailed, that
walked quietly into it, to speak words of peace and

consolation to the dying men whom that terrible storm had beaten down? A smooth-faced stripling, with the Feldpastor's badge on his arm, the gallant Christian son of an eminent Prussian divine, Dr Krummacher of Berlin. At one of the battles (I forget which), a pastor came to fill a grave, not to consecrate it. Shall I ever forget the unswerving hurry to the front of Kummer's divisional chaplain, when the Landwehrleute, his flock, were going down in their ranks, as they held with stubbornness unto death the villages in front of Maizières les Metz? Let the Feldpastoren slobber and welcome, say I, while they gild their slobbering with such devotion as this!

But there must be times and seasons when Herr Pastor is not at hand; nor can the ministration of any pastor stand in the stead of private prayer. The German soldier's simple needs in this way are not disregarded. Each man is served out, when he gets his kit, with a tiny grey volume, less than quarter the size of this page, the title of which is "Gebetbuch für Soldaten"—the Soldier's Prayer-Book. It is supplied from the Berlin depôt of the Head Society for the Promotion of Christian Knowledge in Germany, and is a compendium of simple war-prayers for almost every conceivable situation, with one significant exception—there is no prayer in defeat. The word is blotted out of the German war vocabulary. It has been said that the belief in the divinity of our Saviour is rapidly on the wane in Germany. If this War Prayer-Book avails aught, the taint of the heresy may not enter into the army.

Germany is at war. While Paris is frantically

shouting "À Berlin!" while all Germany is singing
and meaning "Die Wacht am Rhein," Moltke's order
goes forth into the towns and villages for the mobilisation of the Reserve.   Hans was singing "Die
Wacht am Rhein" last night over his beer; but
there is little heart for song left in him as he looks
from that paper on the deal table into Gretchen's face.
She is weeping bitterly as her children cling around
her, too young to realise the cause of their parents'
sorrow.   Hans rises moodily, and pulling down what
military belongings he has not given into the arsenal
after the last drill, falls a turning over of them
abstractedly.   Somehow his hand rests upon the little
grey volume, the "Gebetbuch für Soldaten." It opens
in his hand, and he comes and sits down by Gretchen
and reads, in a voice that chokes sometimes, we may
be sure, the

PRAYER IN STRAIT AND SORROW.

O Lord Jesus Christ! let the crying and sighing of the poor
come before Thee! Withhold not Thy countenance from the
tears and beseechings of the wobegone.   Help by Thine out-
stretched arm, and avert our sorrow from us.   Awake us who
are lying dead in sin and in great danger, and whose thoughts
often wander from thee.   Let us trust with all our hearts that
nothing can be so broad, so deep, so high, nor so arduous that
Thy grace and favour cannot overcome it; that we so can and
must be holpen out of every difficulty and discomfiture when
Thou takest compassion upon us.   Help us, then, through grace,
and so I will praise Thee from now to all eternity.

Hans has bidden good-bye to Gretchen, and kissed
the children he may never see more.   He has marched
with his fellows to the depôt, and got his uniform and
arms.   The *Militärzug* has carried him to Kreuznach,
and thence he has marched sturdily up the Nahe
Valley and over the ridge into the Kollerthaler Wald.

His last halt was at Puttingen, but Kameke has sent an aide back at the gallop to summon up all supports. The regiment stacks arms for ten minutes' breathing-time, the *Kanonendonner* in its ears borne backward on the wind. In two hours more it will be in Frankreich, storming furiously up the Spicheren Berg. As Hans gropes in his tunic pocket for the tinder-box, the little War Prayer-Book somehow gets between his fingers. He takes it out with the pipe-light, and finds in its pages a prayer surely suited to the situation; the prayer

FOR THE OUTMARCHING.

O gracious God! I defile from out my fatherland and from the society of my friends,* and out of the house of my father into a strange land, to campaign against the enemies of our king. Therefore I would cast myself with life and soul upon Thy divine bosom and guardianship; and I pray Thee, with prostrate humility, that Thou wouldst guide me with Thine eye, and overshadow me with Thy wings. Let Thine angels camp round about me, and Thy grace protect me in all the difficulties of the marches, in all camps and dangers. Give me wisdom and understanding for my ways and works. Give success and blessing to our ingoings and outcomings, so that we may do everything well, and conquer on the field of battle; and after victory won, turn our steps homeward as the heralds who announce peace. So shall we praise Thee with gladsomeness, O most gracious Father, for Thy dear Son's sake, Jesus Christ!

It is the morning of Gravelotte. King Wilhelm has issued his laconic order for the day, and all know how bloody and arduous is the task before his host. The French tents are visible away in the distance by

---

* Every now and then you come across a German word untranslatable in its compact volume of expressiveness. How weakly am I forced to render *Freundschaft* here! "Outmarching," though a literal, is a poor equivalent for *Ausmarsch*. In the old Scottish language we find an exact correspondent for *aus*; the "Furthmarch" gives you the idea to a hair's-breadth.

the auberge of St Hubert, and already the explosion
of an occasional shell gives earnest of the wrath to
come.   The regiment in which Hans is a private has
marched to Caulre Farm, and is halted for breakfast
there, before beginning the real battle by attacking
the French outpost-stronghold in Verneville.   The
tough ration-beef sticks in poor Hans' throat.   He
is no coward, but he thinks of Gretchen and the
children, and the Reserve-man draws aside into the
thicket to commune with his own thoughts.   He has
already found comforting thoughts in the little grey
volume, and so he pulls it out again to search for
consolation in this hour of gloom.   He finds what he
wants in the prayer—

FOR THE BATTLE.

Lord of Sabaoth, with Thee is no distinction in helping in great
things or in small.   We are going now, at the orders of our
commanders, to do battle in the field with our enemies.   Let
us give proof of Thy might and honour.   Help us, Lord our
God, for we trust in Thee, and in Thy name we go forth against
the enemy.   Lord Christ, Thou hast said, "I am with thee in
the hour of need: I will pull thee out, and place thee in an
honourable place."   Bethink Thee, Lord, of Thy word, and
remember Thy promise.   Come to our aid when we are sore
pressed, when the close grapple is imminent, when the enemy
overmatches us, and we have been surrounded by them.   Stand
by us in need, for the aid of man is of no avail.   Through Thee
we will vanquish our enemies, and in Thy name we will tread
under the foot those who have set themselves in array against
us.   They trust in their own might, and are puffed up with
pride: but we put our trust in the Almighty God, who, without
one stroke of the sword, canst smite into the dust not only those
who are now formed up against us, but also the whole world.
God, we await on Thy goodness.   Blessed are those who put
their trust in Thee.   Help us, that our enemies may not get the
better of us, and wax triumphant in their might; but strike dis-
order into their ranks, and smite them before our eyes, so that
we may overwhelm them.   Show us Thy goodness, Thou Saviour

of those who trust in thee. Art Thou not God the Lord unto us who are called after Thy name? So be gracious unto us, and take us—life and soul—under the protection of Thy grace. And since Thou only knowest what is good for us, so we commend ourselves unto Thee without reserve, be it for life or for death. Let us live comforted; let us fight and endure comforted; let us die comforted, for Jesus Christ, Thy dear Son's sake. Amen.

Alvensleben is sitting on his horse in the little market-place of Vionville, pulling his grey moustache, and praying that he might see the "Spitze" of Barneckow's division show itself on the edge of the plain to the southward. Rheinbaben's cavalry are half of them down, the other half of them are rallying for another charge, to save the German centre. Hans is in the wood to the north, helping to keep back Lebœuf from swamping the left flank. The shells from the French artillery on the Roman Road are crashing into the wood. The bark is jagged by the cuts of venomous chassepot bullets. Twice has Lebœuf come raging down from the heights of Bruville, twice has he been sent staggering back. Now, with strong reinforcements, he is preparing for a third assault. Meanwhile there is a lull. Hans, grimmed and powder-blackened, may let the breech of his *Zündnadelgewehr* cool, and wipe his bloody bayonet on the forest moss. He has a moment for a glance into the little grey volume, and it opens in his blackened fingers at the prayer—

IN THE AGONY OF THE BATTLE.

O thou Lord and Ruler of Thine own people, awake and look now in grace upon Thy folk. Lord Jesus Christ, be now our Jesus, our helper and deliverer, our rock and fortress, our fiery wall, for Thy great name's sake. Be now our Emmanuel, God with us, God in us, God for us, God by the side of us. Thou mighty arm of Thy Father, let us now see Thy great power, so that men shall hail Thee their God, and the people may bend their knees unto Thee. Strengthen and guide the fighting arm of Thy believing soldiers, and help them, Thou invincible King of Battles. Gird Thyself up, Thou mighty fighting Hero; gird Thy sword on Thy loins, and smite our enemy hip and thigh. Art Thou not the Lord who directest the wars of the whole world, who breakest the bow, who splinterest the spear, and burnest the chariots with fire? Arouse Thyself, help us for Thy good will, and cast us not from Thee, God of our Saviour: cease Thy wrath against us, and think not for ever of our sins. Consider that we are all Thine handiwork; give us Thy countenance again, and be gracious to us. Return unto us, O Lord, and go forth with our army. Restore happiness to us with Thy help and counsel, Thou staunch and only King of Peace, who with Thy suffering and death hast procured for us eternal peace. Give us the victory and an honourable peace, and remain with us in life and in death. Amen.

Hans has marched from Metz towards the valley of the Meuse, and the regimental camp for the night is on the slopes of the Argonne, over against Chemery. The setting sun is glinting on the windows of the Château of Vendresse, where the German King is quartered for the night. The birds are chirruping in the bosky dales of the Bar. The morrow is fraught with the hot struggle of Sedan, but honest Hans, a simple private-man, knows nought of strategic moves, and takes his ease on the sward while he may. He has oiled the needle-gun, and done his cooking; a stone is under his head, and his mantle is about him. As he ponders in the dying rays of the setting sun, there comes over him the impulse to have a look into the pages of the Gebetbuch, and he finds there this prayer :—

FOR THE FIELD ENCAMPMENT.

Heavenly Father, here I am, according to Thy divine will, in the service of my king and war-master, as is my duty as a soldier; and I thank Thee for Thy grace and mercy that Thou hast called me to the performance of this duty, because I am certain that it is not a sin, but is an obedience to Thy wish and will. But as I know and have learnt through Thy gracious Word that none of our good works can avail us, and that nobody can be saved merely as a soldier, but only as a Christian, I will not rely on my obedience and upon my labours, but will perform my duties for Thy sake and to Thy service. I believe with all my heart that the innocent blood of Thy dear Son Jesus Christ, which He has shed for me, delivers and saves me, for He was obedient to Thee even unto death. On this I rely, on this I live and die, on this I fight, and on this I do all things. Retain and increase, O God my Father, this belief by Thy Holy Ghost. I commend body and soul to Thy hands. Amen.

It is the evening of Sedan, the most stupendous victory of the century. The bivouac fires light up the sluggish waters of the Meuse, hardly yet run clear from blood. The burnt villages still smoke on the lower slopes of the Ardennes, and the tired victors, as they point to the beleaguered town, exclaim, in a kind of maze of sober triumph, " Der Kaiser ist da ! " Hans is joyous with his fellows, and as the watch-fire burns up he rummages in the Gebetbuch for something that will chime with the current of his thoughts. He finds it in the prayer for

AFTER THE VICTORY.

God of armies ! Thou hast given us success and victory against our enemies, and hast put them to flight before us. Not unto us, O Lord, not unto us, but to Thy holy name alone be all the honour ! Thou hast done great things for us, therefore our hearts are glad. Without Thy aid we should have been worsted ; only with God could we have done mighty deeds and subdued the power of the enemy. The eye of our General Thou hast quickened and guided ; Thou hast strengthened the courage of our army, and lent it stubborn valour. Yet not the strategy of our leader nor our courage, but Thy great mercy has given us the victory. Lord, who are we, that we dare to stand before Thee as soldiers, and that our enemies yield and fly before us ? We are sinners, even as they are, and have deserved Thy fierce wrath and punishment ; but for the sake of Thy name Thou

hast been merciful to us, and hast so marked the sore peril of
our threatened Fatherland ; and hast heard the prayer of our
king, our people, and our army, because we called upon Thy
name, and held out our buckler in the name of the Lord of Sabaoth. Blessed be Thy holy name for ever and ever.   Amen.

The surrender of the Army of Sedan has been consummated ; and Hans, marching down by Rethel,
and through grand old Rheims, and along the
smiling vinebergs of the Marne valley, is now "vor
Paris."   He is on the Feldwache, in the forest of
Bondy, before Rainey, and his turn comes to go on
the uttermost sentry-post. As the snow-drift blows
to one side, he can see the French watch-fires close
by him in Bondy ; nearer still, he sees the three
stones and the few spadefuls of earth behind which,
as he knows, is the French outpost sentry confronting
him.   The straggling rays of the watery moon, now
obscured by snow-scud, now falling on him faintly,
could not aid him in reading, even if he dared avert
his eyes from his front. But Hans has learned the
value of the little grey volume ; and while he lay in
the Feldwache waiting for his spell of sentry go, he
had learnt by heart the following prayer :—

FOR OUTPOST SENTRY DUTY.

Lord Jesus Christ, I stand here on the foremost fringe of the
camp, and am holding watch against the enemy ; but wert Thou,
Lord, not to guard us, then the watcher watcheth in vain.
Therefore, I pray Thee, cover us with Thy grace as with a
shield, and let Thy holy angels be round about us to guard and
preserve us that we be not fallen upon at unawares by the
enemy. Let the darkness of the night not terrify me ; open
mine eyes and ears that I may observe the oncoming of the
enemy from afar, and that I may study well the care of myself
and of the whole army.   Keep me in my duty from sleeping on
my post and from false security.   Let me continually call to
Thee with my heart, and bend Thyself unto me with Thine

almighty presence. Be Thou with me and strengthen me, life and soul, that in frost, in heat, in rain, in snow, in all storms, I may retain my strength and return in health to the Feldwache. So I will praise Thy name and laud Thy protection. Amen.

It is the evening of the 2d of December. Trochu has tried his hardest to sup in Lagny, and has been baulked by German valour. But not without terrible loss. On the plateau, and by the park wall before Villiers, dead and wounded Germans lie very thick. In one of the little corries in the vineberg poor Hans has gone down. The shells from Fort Nogent are bursting all around, deterring the Krankenträger from prosecuting their functions. Hans has somehow bound up his shattered limb; and as he pulled his handkerchief from his pocket, the little Gebetbuch dropped out with it. There are none on earth to comfort poor Hans ; let him open the book and find consolation there in the prayer—

FOR THE SICK AND WOUNDED.

Dear and trusty Deliverer, Jesus Christ, I know in my necessity and pains no whither to flee to but to Thee, my Saviour, who hast suffered for me, and hast called unto all ailing and miserable ones, " Come unto me, all ye who are weary and heavy-laden, and I will give you rest." Oh relieve me also, of Thy love and kindness, stretch out Thy healing and almighty hand, and restore me to health. Free me with Thy aid from my disease and my pains, and console me with Thy grace who art vouchsafed to heal the broken heart, and to console all the sorrowful ones. Dost Thou take pleasure in our destruction ? our groaning touches Thee to the heart, and those whom Thou hast cast down Thou wilt lift up again. In Thee, Lord Jesus, I put my trust ; I will not cease to importune Thee that Thou bringest me not to shame. Help me, save me, so I will praise Thee for ever. Amen.

Alas for Gretchen and her brood ! The 4th of December has dawned, and still Hans lies unfound in the corry of the vineberg. He has no pain now, for his shattered limb has been numbed by the cruel frost. His eyes are waxing dim, and he feels the end near at hand. The foul raven of the battlefield croaks above him in his lonely sequestration, impatient for its meal. The grim king of terrors is very close to thee, poor honest soldier of the Fatherland ; but thou canst face him as boldly as thou hast faced the foe, with the help of the little book of which thy frost-chilled fingers have never lost the grip. He falls back as thou murmurest the prayer—

AT THE NEAR APPROACH OF DEATH.

Merciful heavenly Father, Thou God of all consolation, I thank Thee that Thou hast sent Thy dear Son Jesus Christ to die for me. He has through His death taken from death his sting, so that I have no cause to fear him more. In that I thank Thee, dear Father, and pray Thee receive my spirit in grace, as it now parts from life. Stand by me and hold me with Thine almighty hand, that I may conquer all the terrors of death. When my ears can hear no more, let Thy Spirit commune with my spirit, that I, as Thy child and co-heir with Christ, may speedily be with Jesus by Thee in heaven. When my eyes can see no more, so open my eyes of faith that I may then see Thy heaven open before me and the Lord Jesus on Thy right hand ; that I may also be where He is. When my tongue shall refuse its utterance, then let Thy Spirit be my spokesman with indescribable breathings, and teach me to say with my heart, "Father, into Thy hands I commit my spirit." Hear me, for Jesus Christ's sake. Amen.

Would it harm the British soldier, think you, if in his kit there was a " Gebetbuch für Soldaten ?"

FLOGGED.

FLOGGED.[*]

I AM a highly respectable man now, as the world goes. I have a balance at my banker's, and round my mahogany I have occasionally the honour of entertaining a company of highly eligible acquaintances. I have even attained to the dignity of having a toady, who professes to be impressed with the most profound surprise that I should retain a carriage so upright, and that the manifold cares of business and the practice of stooping over papers should not have had the effect of detracting from the squareness of my shoulders or diminished the development of my chest. The fellow little knows to what I am indebted for those physical characteristics. He little imagines that my shoulders were squared, my chest thrown out, and my figure generally set up by a course of calisthenics known as "suppling motions," the tutor being a whiskered monster of a drill-sergeant, with a voice emanating from the region of the diaphragm, and the

[*] This paper was written before the abolition of the use of the lash in the army. The story it narrates is a perfectly true tale. The facts, and the sensations under the "cat," were narrated to me by the person to whom the experience told in the article occurred, and as to the truth of whose statements, so far as they related to questions of fact, I had additional confirmation.

pupil myself in the ignoble character of a raw recruit.
Perhaps his flattery would not be so profuse if he knew
this, or if he could stomach this piece of information.
I think, were he to know that the man to whom he is
so lavishly sycophantish had actually in his time been
the recipient of fifty lashes with the cat-o'-nine-tails,
and that at the present time he carries about with him
between his shoulders certain long blue and red cica-
trices which the vulgar call weals—I think, I say, that
even this persistent toady would recoil from his task
with dismay.   Yes, reader, I am telling the simple
truth ; though my coat is good, my linen irreproach-
able, my outward *tout ensemble* quite that of the prosperous British citizen, my back is scored and branded
with the imprint of the cat.

I go down in the orthodox way every autumn to some
seaside haunt or other, and folks wonder why I never
bathe.   There is an excellent reason.   Messieurs the
farriers of the —— Regiment of Dragoons were kind
enough to set a mark upon me—not as Cain carried
his, on the forehead, but on the back, and the brand is
indelible, as if it had been seared into the naked flesh
with red-hot irons.   I think it gets deeper the older I
grow.   Sometimes I fancy it is fading, and as I strip
in the seclusion of my own room, and look over my
shoulder at the reflection of my disfigured back in the
mirror, I imagine my flesh is coming again "like the
flesh of a little child."   My face flushes with pleasure
at the thought, and lo ! in damnable unison with the
glow on my cheeks, the blood seems to rush into the
pale weals, the faint discolourations become darker
and empurpled, the whole back bursts into a fiery
blaze, and glows with as much angry redness as on

the day I was discharged from hospital with the laconic
"Healed" scored on my bed-head ticket. I dress
again, and shut my skeleton up in its closet, and go
out and rub shoulders in the busy world with men
whose backs are clean if their hands are dirty. I have
kept my secret well, and nobody suspects me.

I met my old colonel the other day, and was introduced to him by a "mutual friend." He didn't recognise—it wasn't likely—in the prosperous man who
lifted his hat with his gloved hand, the poor rascal over
whom he stood with knitted brow and coldly critical eye
as the farrier's thongs cut into his naked flesh, and
who threatened a tender-hearted operator with "a dose
of the same physic himself if he didn't lay on harder."
I dare say that staunch and truly Briton-like sub-
scriber to the Eyre Defence Fund, next to whom I
once sat at a public dinner, would have drawn his chair
away from mine in blankest dismay had he known that
he was sitting next to a man who had been flogged
just like the "infernal nigger" he talked of to me
with such thorough gusto in the intervals between the
speeches. I make no doubt that fussy and florid
lieutenant-colonel of Foot, who not long ago travelled
with me in the same carriage on the South-Western
line as far as Aldershot—that Gehenna of sand and
drill—and who was so loud and full-mouthed in his
blusterous encomia of "Discipline, sir, discipline;
nothing like blank, good, stiff, sharp punishment for
keeping up the discipline of the service—going to the
dogs, sir, fast, with blank nonsensical rules about first-
class and second-class, and soldiers' gardens, and such
like infernal rot"—I verily believe this bluff disci-
plinaire would have jumped right out of the window

F

had I thought it advisable to shock his bustling com-
placency by taking off my coat and requesting him
to make an inspection of my epidermis in the region
of the shoulders. But I kept my counsel, and let the
wire-cat amateur and the flogging professional make
a block of me on which to air their kindly and genial
hobbies without a wince or a murmur ; and if they
did not get much out of me in the way of appreciative
reply, why, they were notable talkers themselves, and
no doubt set me down as an excellent listener.

When I first re-entered civil life I was full of generous
impulse to make a vigorous crusade against the lash,
which I felt ought to be abhorred by man, as it is ac-
cursed of God ; but I found the great majority of the
world strangely blunt of feeling on the subject, and
that a very large proportion of educated men, who
called themselves enlightened, reasoning, sensible
people, positively had a warm corner in their hearts
for the institution of the cat. Men—men, too, who
professed to have brains and hearts—shrugged their
shoulders and fiddled with their shirt-collars when I
button-holed them on the lash question ; and even
those who sympathised with my sentiments put a
damper on my ardour by the expression of a belief
that the matter was not yet ripe for effectual agita-
tion. I at one time nourished the Quixotic design of
striving for a seat in Parliament, and trying the effect
on the House of the *argumentum ad tergum* by a
theatrical display of the weals on my shoulders, after
the manner of Burke with the dagger ; but such wild
ideas engendered in the solitude of the closet are apt
to fade in the everyday bustling intercourse with the
world, and so it has come to pass that I have fallen

into the habit of considering the "triangle" episode
of my life "as a dream that has been told." Were it
not, indeed, for the convincing evidence I carry about
with me, and the burning sense of wrong and injury
which comes over me when the subject recurs to my
mind, I would at times have difficulty in realising that
I had once in verity been tied up.

I need not narrate the circumstances which led me
to follow the example of many another scapegrace,
and take the Queen's shilling. Being a lissom, smart
young fellow enough, I made a capital dragoon, so
far as *physique* went. I didn't bear a bad character
in the regiment neither; far from it, but was a careless, happy-go-lucky young rascal, taking things just
as they came, and never refused a glass of beer when
it was offered me. So I soldiered away cheerily
enough for some two years, having got into one or two
minor scrapes, certainly, but contriving generally to
keep tolerably clear of the defaulter's book, and with
good credit as a smart, soldierly dragoon. Of course,
soldier-like, I could not do without falling violently in
love in every town we were quartered in, and if my
heart had not been made of a gutta-percha-like substance, it must have broken over and over again at the
sound of our marching-out tune—"The girl I left behind me"—who (the girl, I mean) was probably dis-
consolate, like me, for a period not exceeding three
clear days.

We were lying at the time of my story in these
halcyon quarters for a dragoon regiment, Brighton,
and I, according to use and wont, was head and
ears in love with a pretty little resident in that
town of big houses and bad beer. Sunday afternoon

used to be great occasions with us sprightly blue
jackets, and on one of these I had been enjoying a
beautiful stroll in the company of my sweetheart,
during which the time flitted by so rapidly that it was
close upon the evening stable hour while we were
still in the vicinity of the Pavilion Barracks. After
a deal of persuasion, I prevailed upon my fair companion to enter the barracks, and to remain in the
barrack-room during the hour devoted to wisping,
watering, and bedding down, on the understanding
that when it was over I should escort her home.
Leaving her, accordingly, in the empty room, I
slipped off my jacket, ran down on parade, answered
my name, and accompanied my mates to the
stables.

During the progress of the hour, I found I had
forgotten a necessary grooming implement, and ran
up into the room to fetch it.   On entering it, to
my surprise and anger, I found my little friend crying bitterly, and a hound of a corporal, who had just
come off gate-piquet, standing over her, grinning like
a hyena.   The poor girl, seeing me, jumped up
eagerly, and with a fresh burst of tears ran to claim
my protection, when the lubberly non-commissioned
officer threw his arms round her, trying to force her
back to her seat, at the same time peremptorily ordering me back to the stable.   I didn't go.   Instead of
that I caught him a hot one straight between the eyes,
and dropped him as neatly as if he had been pole-
axed; and then, taking the girl by the arm, I had her
across the passage and into a married soldier's room
in the twinkling of an eye.   There I left her to the
kind attentions of good old Polly Tudor, and then

quietly walked down to the stable again, and set to work wisping my old horse with violent energy, to carry off some of the steam generated by the little episode I have just narrated.

Now, if this corporal had been a man he would not have insulted the girl at all ; if, again, he had been half a man, having done so, and having been justly chastised for his insolence, he would either have owned that it "served him right," or, if he had felt himself aggrieved by the blow, he might have requested the pleasure of my society for a quarter of an hour in the forage-yard, and had a go in for satisfaction. But as it happened, he was no man at all, and therefore, when he had succeeded in picking himself up, and pulling himself together, he followed me down into the stable, and consigned me to the guard-room instantly. It was not till I was fairly locked up and left to myself in the dark cell, that I began to realise the seriousness of my position. I had actually been guilty (and the provocation would not avail me a jot) of the most serious offence a soldier can commit, according to military laws. The penalty for striking a superior officer stands in the code military as "death, or such other punishment as a court-martial may inflict." They don't shoot dragoons now-a-days—but the —— was a flogging regiment, and my spinal marrow curdled again as if the thongs were already slashing me.

Everything was done in rigid accordance with rules. I was duly warned for a district court-martial, and about the middle of the week I was escorted into the presence of the dread Sanhedrim. The adjutant of the regiment was the prosecutor, and my enemy, the

corporal, and his pair of black eyes, the only witnesses against me.   During the interval he had invented a tale which was both ingenious and plausible.
I had, as he testified, introduced a female into the
barrack-room—irregularity number one.   I had left
the stable in the course of the stable hour, and stolen
up into the room to enjoy the lady's society—another
grievous fault.   He had casually entered the room,
found me there, and ordered me out, to which my
only reply was a knock-down blow, which had caused
the certainly beautiful black eyes to which the corporal parenthetically pointed plaintively.   My attempt to refute this plausible tale was simply a farce,
as I was not allowed to cite the only witness who
could have disproved it, nor indeed would the court
have believed her had she confirmed me in every
particular ; so as I went back to the guard-room I
was compelled to coincide in the opinion of one of my
escort, who, in the true spirit of a Job's comforter,
offered to bet me two to one in sixpences I was
"good for fifty."

Yet in the quiet of my cell, the more I tried
to habituate myself to the grim look forward
the worse job I made of it.   I tried to conjure up
the scene—the men drawn up round the riding-
school, the farrier-major standing by the triangle,
then the colonel's deep voice rolling out the para-
graphs of the court-martial proceedings ; and then it
seemed as if I had been doing all this in the case of
somebody else, and that it was not I who was standing there bareheaded and with jacket loose, listening
to the horrible sentence.   Do what I would, I could
not bring the reality home to *myself*; whenever

I tried to concentrate my thoughts on the idea that it was my very self who was to suffer this ignominy, my mind went to pieces, as it were, and the fragments grasped hold of such trivialities as whether the morning would be wet or dry, whether the parade would be a full dress or stable dress one, whether the "Old Doctor" or the assistant surgeon would be present, and such like pitiful details.

Two days passed thus, and on the third morning the sergeant of the guard, after I had washed, instead of ordering me back into the cell, told me to sit down by the guard-room fire and eat my breakfast there. I had no appetite. I saw what was coming in the sergeant's eye, and in the concerned looks of the guard. After I had swallowed a few mouthfuls of coffee, I noticed the sergeant whisper to a man, who went out and presently returned with some spirits in a bottle. "Here, my lad," said the good-hearted old serjeant, "knock this half-pint of rum into you—it will deaden the pain, and make you stick it better." Thoroughly appreciating the kindly motive of the good fellow, I could not bring myself to use his recipe for Dutch courage, it would have been more degrading than the lash itself; so, just wetting my lips, I passed the bottle round, and it did not go far in the cold autumn morning.

By and by the orderly came down with orders from the adjutant for the prisoner to be got ready. The preparation was not an elaborate one. All I had to do was to take my stock and braces off, buckle on a waiststrap, give my cloak to one of the escort to throw over my shoulders after the butchery was over, and then I was ready. In ten minutes more I was in the riding-school, where the triangles were rigged at one end, and a couple of troops drawn up as spectators. The colonel, the adjutant, the doctor, and a few other officers were standing in the centre of the school; and as soon as I was halted within an easy distance of the group, the colonel began to read sonorously the "Proceedings of a district court-martial," &c., &c. He read on uninterruptedly till he came to the word "sentence," when he paused, deliberately folded up the sheets of paper, and then facing me full, said slowly and emphatically, "Fifty lashes and eighty-four days imprisonment." Then raising his voice, he shouted "Strip!"

I would be flogged a dozen times over rather than endure that minute of horrible suspense between the time when, my shirt pulled over my head, my wrists were securely lashed to the triangles, and the colonel's stern voice gave the word "Begin." At last down came the thongs, with an angry whizz, straight and fair on the back, and every nerve in my body gave a bound from my brain to my toes. The actual pain of the lacerated flesh, agony as it was, was nothing compared with the horrible crashing jar on the nerves, and it was this which so taxed my resolution to repress any sign of feeling. Every atom of my whole body seemed imbued with a separate palpitating, throbbing existence—the whole muscular system thrilled and vibrated with a convulsive agony. Another blow higher up, and every nerve gave a fresh stab and shoot, as if it would crack. "Three!"—still a wilder quiver shot through me, and I had to clench my lower lip desperately between my teeth, or I could not have restrained the convulsive impulse to call out.

There is no need for detailing further the horrible
sensations I endured; suffice it to say, that after
the first dozen lashes a feeling of bluntness and
deadness came over the nervous system; and I really
believe, so far as my own experience goes, that after
this, provided the bodily energy is strong enough to
bear up against the nervous strain, it matters but
little whether twenty or fifty lashes are inflicted. I
have heard men say that every fragment of lacerated
flesh became excruciatingly and agonisingly sensitive; but my experience does not bear this out. By
the time I had received twenty lashes, though I had
desperate difficulty to conquer a growing, faintish
nausea which came over me, I was not conscious of
suffering any actual poignant agony. I could feel
each lash as it fell, but it seemed to fall upon numbed
—I would almost say frozen—flesh; and the feeling
was not so much of laceration as of blunt blows from
a stick, bruising rather than cutting. But I could
feel the tension of the nervous system growing tighter
and tighter, and seeming to concentrate itself on the
crown of the head, and to corrugate the very skull,
and then a feeling of deadly faintness would all but
master me, and I would find myself wishing that the
lash would happen to fall upon a fresh spot, so that
the new thrill of pain might keep me from becoming
insensible. At length, when hours had apparently
elapsed, I heard, dreamily and faintly, the word "Fifty."
The knife was applied to the thongs which bound my
wrists; with a hard effort I straightened myself up,
pulled my shirt over my back with my own hands,
threw unassisted the cloak over my shoulders, and
took my place between the files forming my escort.

I just managed to reach the hospital before I fainted. There I remained about ten days under the doctor's hands, and then was committed to the military prison to serve out my term of imprisonment. More fortunate than many a poor fellow, I was spared the shame of looking men in the face who had seen me beaten like a hound. When my term of imprisonment was over, I was brought back to my regiment under escort, conducted straight to the orderly-room, and there told that I was a free man, that my discharge had been obtained through some special influence, and that I might leave the regiment and the service the same day. I was out of barracks and in civilian's clothes in an hour's time. This is the history of how I came to be "flogged."

A SUNDAY AFTERNOON AT GUY'S.

A SUNDAY AFTERNOON AT GUY'S.

WE ought all to go to church on Sunday afternoon, I
know. There can't be a doubt, I take it, that the
theory is quite right; but somehow in the summer-
time the practice is not so easy. The forenoon service, no matter how hot the weather is, can be
sustained and enjoyed in defiance of soporific influences, and the evening ordinance is that chiefly
effected by preachers worth hearing. But the curate
is mostly thought good enough for the thin attendance of the afternoon, and the temptation to a *siesta*,
although confessedly reprehensible, is almost irresistible. And I think it just possible in such a vast
kaleidoscope as London to find here and there a scene
where a Sunday afternoon may be spent to almost as
much substantial edification, if it only be looked
at in the right spirit, as within the orthodox walls of
a church. Such an one came under my eye one
Sunday afternoon, "over the water;" and, without
pretending to "see sermons in stones," I think what
I witnessed did me very nearly as much good as if I
had been listening to the curate.

Most of us are pretty well acquainted with the
characteristics of London Bridge. But many a Lon-

93

doner may cross the bridge every day without thinking of turning down an unambitious street which
opens up on the left a little way on the Surrey side
of it. St Thomas Street is the name it bears, from
the hospital of the same name which used to flank it,
but the site of which is now a chaos of waste-land,
bricks and mortar, and half-built houses. On a week-
day this street is quiet—without much fear of contra-
diction, I might say dull—its leading indigenous
productions seemingly being arches, doctors, hoard-
ings, and railway clerks. But the scene on Sunday
afternoon, from two to four, is in marked contrast to
the week-day aspect of the thoroughfare. A multitude of costermongers' barrows line the pathway,
laden with the dainties which are in season—cherries,
strawberries, oranges, ginger beer, and hardbake,
being the chief vendibles on the occasion of my visit.
And they drive a roaring trade these peripatetic
fruiterers, for crowds of persons, some well-dressed,
some clad very humbly, men, women, and children,
all seem to consider it a duty to make an investment
with one or other of the barrow owners as they pass.
I say pass, but they don't pass : one and all have the
same goal, which is a pair of large iron gates opening
into the thoroughfare directly opposite where the
press of costermongers is thickest. Through the gates
they keep entering unremittingly—now in twos and
threes, now quite a little throng—and as the hands of
the clock point nearer to three, there seems hardly
room enough between the massive pillars for the crowd.

It is the great forecourt of the famous Guy's Hospital to which these gates form the ingress, and this
Sunday afternoon's multitude is the throng of visitors

to patients lying ill within the precincts of the mighty hospital. The hours of admission are from two to four, and during that time it is computed that from two to three thousand persons visit friends within. The figures may seem startling, but then it must be remembered that this great charity contains something like six hundred and fifty beds, and that London clamours eagerly for every vacancy, so that the proportion of visitors to patients is not so much out of the way. The building is a vast one, consisting of a great forecourt enclosed on three sides by lofty buildings, a large interior court wholly built round, a second huge detached building down on the garden—a respectable hospital in itself—and several wards besides standing about the garden rather promiscuously.

The dispensary and public offices of the hospital confront us as we ascend the steps out of the forecourt, and passing a little further on we come to the great accident ward on the left, placed thus close to the entrance to spare as much as possible the needless transport of the grievously injured. When we read of some dire accident in the southern part of London, the concluding sentence of the paragraph generally informs us that "the injured were conveyed to Guy's Hospital," and then it is ten to one we think no more about it. But here, many months after, you will find some sad mementoes of the occurrence in the shape of men slowly recovering from hurts all but fatal, and the traditions of stupendous accidents linger long about this ward, and form the mental milestones of the sisters and nurses, just as sportsmen talk of Thormanby's or Lord Lyon's year.

On this particular afternoon, the demon of accident having been comparatively still for some time previous, the accident ward was not so sensational as usual. In a bed next the door sat upright, cheerily chatting to his brother, a bright young shaver, whose knee-cap had been smashed by a sudden eccentric gyration of his peg-top; but the worst of the little lad's trouble was over, and he was looking forward to a speedy removal home. Next to him lay desolate a friendless old man, whose hand had been amputated but the day before. A comforting word from a friend might have soothed the pain he manifestly endured, but nobody came to say it, and so he bore his heavy cross in mournful silence. Further down the ward a great-limbed powerful fellow lay helplessly comatose and insensible. But a day or two before he had come down by the run along with a massive girder, and the result was a concussion of the brain. There he lay, neither dead nor alive, and by the bed-head sat a weather-beaten, anxious-eyed woman, with a couple of poorly-clad but clean boys, gazing in silent desolation at the husband, father, and bread-winner, who might never speak again. Opposite this cot, again, was a blithe sailor lad, who had tumbled down a ship's hold and got smashed into pieces, but with the proverbial luck of sailor boys, had got mended again, and was now anxiously waiting for the captain of his ship to come and claim him.

The convalescent ground, which we reached after traversing the main building, is a pleasant, shady place, full of trees and flowers, and it is a curious study. The folks who are allowed to leave the wards and take out-door exercise frequent it, and some

extraordinary specimens of humanity in the curative
stage may be seen in different parts of it. Here is a
man, both of whose arms have been broken, and they
are now undergoing the process of being mended,
flattened out on a couple of boards upon which the
limbs are bandaged down, giving him a strange joint-
less look, as if he had exchanged the human arm for
the flippers of a turtle. Other men are limping about
on crutches, with a leg in splints, supported by a
strap round the neck, something on the principle of
the dumb jockey with which horsebreakers use to
give colts a mouth. And here and there, again, are
people, seemingly sound and whole, sitting on the
benches underneath the verdant trees, and you wonder what such as they do in an hospital for the sick ;
but come closer, and look at the pale, wasted face,
with the hectic plague-spot of consumption on the
thin cheek, and if you sit down beside them, you feel
the solid seat vibrate again with the violence of the
racking cough which rends the decaying lungs.

The children are the greatest and best of the many
studies which the place affords. Here and there you
will find one manifestly dying, with the destroyer's
seal imprinted unmistakably on the pallid little face
and wasted limbs, as the blighted bud lies languidly
withering away from the bright world, heedless of the
singing of the birds on the boughs outside, mindless
of the balmy sunshine and the fresh breeze which
permeates everywhere, thinking even the presence of
friends an irksome burden, a weariness of the flesh,
and anxious apparently only to be left alone to fade
away in utter quiet. But mostly the urchins have
got round the ugly corner of their illness or their

G

accident, and are cockily recovering with all convenient speed. They are the true autocrats of their
ward, the pet of the sisters, the amusement of the
seniors, and generally the life and light of the whole
place. Some of them are holding quite a levée
round their blue-striped divans, considering themselves evidently in the light of experienced veterans
who have safely emerged from the rocks and shallows
of outrageous fortune, and are condescendingly
patronising to their parental relatives, positively
astounding in their calm insolence to the ordinarily
formidable maiden aunt, and flatly giving the cut
direct to elder brothers and sisters, who are quite
chickens in the ways of the world, for they have not
been inmates of Guy's. Just listen to the ineffable
tone of superiority in which this promising six-year-
old is enlightening his pleased but slightly puzzled
family as to the regulations of the hospital, the doctors, the chaplains, the sisters, the diet ; and jabber-
ing the technicalities, which are of course household
words in the hospital, with a triumphant remorseless-
ness quite comical to hear. And in truth some of the
prelections of this young gentleman are sufficiently
puzzling to an outsider, for he keeps talking of Sister
Naaman and Sister Job in à free and easy style quite
bewildering to anybody with settled ideas on the subject of gender. Now I had always associated the
name of Naaman with an individual of the male sex,
and my conviction hitherto had been that Job was a
patriarch, and therefore a man. The explanation of
the little puzzle is, that the different wards are mostly
christened by some notable Scripture name, such as
Dorcas, Lydia, Esther, Job, Naaman, &c., and the

sister or nurse in charge of each abandons her own patronymic, and assumes instead as a surname the title of her ward. Hence Sister Naaman, Sister Abraham, and so forth. How inexpressibly tender and pleasant is this word "sister," as used in this sense—what an endearing feeling of relationship it conveys between nurse and patient ! It is the touch of nature which makes the little world of the ward akin.

We find all classes of patients here, and, as a consequence, all classes of visitors. Well-dressed men in black frock coats and seeming ladies in fashionable bonnets and handsome dresses surround one bed, while corduroy and moleskin sit about the next. Caste is not studied at Guy's. The grave is said to obliterate all distinction, but one may fancy the hospital ward quite as effectual a leveller. Names are abrogated in favour of numbers ; and were a peer of the realm to be admitted as an inmate, he would have to leave his title outside the gate, and be known in the ward solely and only as No. 6 or No. 8. What is more, I verily believe that if the said peer were only what, in hospital parlance, is called a "slight case," the bricklayer's labourer in the next bed, with the miscellaneously smashed carcase, would monopolise so much of the sister's care as to necessitate the aristocrat's attending to his own comfort, always supposing that the nature of his malady permitted.

Here, where Whig and Tory, tatterdemalion and compound householder, find the same level under the universal prebald counterpane, the chief ambition seems to be in a position to sing with Mr Toole, in the " Artful Dodger," " My circle of acquaintance, I'm

proud to say, is great," as developed in a large number
of visitors round the cot. Some are very fortunate in
this respect, holding quite a reception to a succession
of visitors, laden with the succulent dainties of the
costers' barrows I saw outside the gate. Other
patients, again, have a more limited acquaintance,
only one or two visitors being seated by their bed-
sides ; but it is mostly noticeable that the earnestness
and solicitude for the patient's welfare is in the inverse ratio to the number of visitors. Thus, while
here and there we find but a single visitor, be sure he
or she sits by the bedhead, bending lovingly over the
recumbent relative, and whispering earnestly scraps
of home intelligence and words of tender encouragement. A wife, mayhap, telling the sick husband
bravely how well the humble household is getting on
without the breadwinner, when her anxious eye and
pinched face belie the courageous words; a mother
telling her boy how his homecoming is looked forward to ; or a stalwart young fellow trying to gal-
vanise the thin blood of a white-haired father, who
will never again, the death-look in the old man's face
tells me, lean on the manly arm of his lad.

Perhaps the very saddest spectacle of all is to see
the utterly friendless. Thank God, there are not a
great many of them ; but here and there lies a poor
desolate fellow, who owns nobody in this stony-
hearted solitude of London to say "God speed" to
him. They lie, these forlorn ones, with sad, longing
eye, listening for a scrap of humanising conversation
which is going on around them—how eager to respond to a kind word, how grateful if you will but sit
down by them for a minute, and spend on them a

little cheap interest. Yokels—a proportion of these —heavy labouring men from Devon or Yorkshire, stolid of face, and clownish of accent, who have fallen upon accident or sickness up in London here, and have found Guy's act the good Samaritan. Others of the forlorn are foreigners, men of colour some of them—one or two to whom I spoke all but utterly ignorant of the English tongue, and probably without a single friend but Guy's within the four corners of the land. But black or white, Jew or Gentile, Greek or Barbarian, all have the same treatment here; the pleasant-faced sister has the same kindly attention for all; the best doctors in Europe equally spend their best knowledge and experience.

Sitting out here in the convalescent ground in the pleasant sunshine, listening to the animated conversation of a batch of our irrepressible friends of the Emerald Isle, to whom a gentleman, who bears the visible imprints of a poker about his visage, is illustrating, with diagrams, the correct history of the Tooley Street shindy, in which "me own sisther's son's wife's brother" cracked his crown, one is apt to forget that he is within the precincts of an hospital at all. But here comes a grim reminder. A rough wooden shell, supported by a porter at either end, is borne slowly towards us; the impressible Irish hush their prate as the poor relic of humanity is carried past them, and we start with something like dismay to find our pleasant seat has been within a yard or two of the iron wicket which leads to the deadhouse. A minute later, and the bell rings, warning visitors that their time is up. Then the tide of humanity sets outward with as much briskness as an hour and a half ago it was setting inward; and as I mingle with the throng I ask myself the question, whether my Sunday afternoon has not been spent as profitably, for once in a way, as in listening to a sermon.

BUTCHER JACK'S STORY.

BUTCHER JACK'S STORY.

IT was in the autumn of 1854 that the English and French armies were lying lovingly enough together in front of Sebastopol, that nut which it took them such a time to crack. Our cavalry had a camp of their own upon the hill-side near Kadikoi, and the old "Death's-head and Cross-bones," to which I belonged, were there among the rest, forming part of the Light Brigade. We had a separate commissary of our own, and handy men were told off from the various corps to act as butchers. I never was backward when there was any work to do; and when some fellows were moping helplessly in the tents, or going sick to hospital, every morning I was knocking about as jolly as a sandboy, doing a job here and one there, and always contriving to get more or less tipsy before nightfall. If you ever drop across any of the old Crimean Light Brigade, just you ask them if they remember "Butcher Jack" of the Lancers, and see what the answer will be. I was as well known in the Brigade as old Cardigan himself, and in my rough-and-tumble way got to be quite a popular character. Indeed, had it not been for my inordinate fondness for the drink, I might have got promotion over and over again.   But I used to find my way shoulder-high into the guard-tent pretty regularly once a week, and more than once I only saved the skin of my back by being known as a willing, useful fellow when sober.

One "slaughtering day" at the Commissary we had killed, flayed, and cut up our number of beasts, and there was a lot of rum knocking about, for the Commissary Guard knew how to get at the grog, and were free enough with it among the butchers, for the sake of a nice tender steak.   Paddy Heffernan, of the Royals, and I, managed to get as drunk as lords before we found time for a wash, and one of the Commissary-officers came across us while in this state, and clapped us in the guard-tent before you could say "knife."   One place was as good as another to us, so we lay there contented enough all night, taking an occasional tot out of a bottle which Paddy managed to smuggle into the tent where we were confined.   It was getting on for morning before we dropped off into a heavy, drunken sleep, out of which the Commander-in-Chief himself would have had a tough job to have roused us.   We must have had a long snooze, for it was broad daylight before we were wakened by the loud thundering of a tremendous cannonade close by, making the very tent-poles quiver again.

I still felt deucedly muzzy, for Commissary rum, as you would know if you ever got tight on it, is hard stuff to get sober off, yet I managed to pull myself together enough to know where I was, and could give a shrewd guess what all the row was.   I sat up with the intention of hearing more

about it from some of the guard; but to my surprise
there was not a soul in the tent but Paddy and myself, and there was not even a sentry upon the door.
So we both got up on end and had a stretch, and
then walked coolly out of the guard-tent, only to find
the camp utterly deserted, not a man being apparently left in it.

Turning into our own tent, we sat down, and
over a refresher out of the inexhaustible rum
bottle, we tried, in a boozy sort of way, to argue
out the position. From where the camp was we
could not see what was going on down in the valley
by reason of a low ridge which intercepted the view;
but we could tell it must be pretty warm work, from
the hot and continuous firing which was being kept
up. At last says I to Paddy, "Why the devil should
we be out of the fun? Let's go up to the sick horse
lines, and see if there be anything left there fit to put
one leg in front of another." "Agreed," cries he,
heartily enough; so I got hold of a butcher's axe for
a weapon, and he a sword, and, half-drunk as we
were, and just in the condition we had left off killing
the night before, we started off for the sick horses.
But it was no go for a moment here, for there were
but two brutes left, and one of them had a leg like a
pillar letter-box, while the other was down on his
side, and did not look much like rising again. Determined not to be beaten, we started off on foot, and
making our way round by the rear of the staff, who
were on the edge of the little ridge, we dodged down
into the valley just in the rear of the position of the
heavy cavalry.

Fill the pot again, governor, and I may as well

tell you it was Balaclava morning, and the heavies had
already charged the Russian cavalry, and emptied a
good many saddles.   Russian horses were galloping
about riderless, and Paddy and myself parted company to give chase to a couple of these.   With some
trouble I captured my one, a tidy little iron-grey nag,
which I judged from the saddle and accoutrements
must have been an officer's charger.   It was easy to
see from the state of the saddle that the former rider
had been desperately wounded, and the reins too
were bloodier than a dainty man would have liked ;
but I was noways squeamish, and mounted the little
horse in a twinkling.   The moment I had got my
seat, I galloped up to the Heavy Brigade, and formed
up coolly on the left flank of the old Royals.   They
laughed at me as if I had been a clown in a panto-
mime ; and I had not been in position a couple of
minutes when up came Johnny Lee, their adjutant,
on his old bay mare, at a tearing gallop, and roared
to me to "Go to h—— out of that."   There 's no mistake, I was not much of a credit to them.   I was
bareheaded, and my hair was like a birch-broom in a
fit.   I was minus a coat, with my shirt-sleeves turned
up to the shoulder, and my shirt, face, and bare hairy
arms were all splashed and barkened with blood,
which I had picked up at the butchering the day
before, and had never wiped off.   A pair of long,
greasy jack-boots came up to the thigh, and instead
of a sword I had the axe over my shoulder at the
slope as regimental as you please.   The Russian must
have ridden very short, for my knees were up to my
nose in his stirrups, and so you may imagine that,
taking me all in all, I was rather a hot-looking mem-

ber, especially if you remember that I was fully half-seas over.

The heavies were in position to support the Light Brigade, which had just got the word to advance. So when the adjutant of the Royals ordered me off, I looked straight before me, and saw the light bobs going out to the front at an easy trot, and on the right of the front rank I caught sight of the plumes in the lance hats of my own corps, the old seventeenth. My mind was made up on the instant. Ramming my spurless heels into the ribs of the little Russian horse, I started off in pursuit of the Light Brigade as fast as I could make him go, with shouts of laughter from the heavies ringing behind me, and chased unsuccessfully by a couple of officers of the Greys, who tried to stop me for decency's sake.

As the light bobs were only advancing at the trot, I wasn't long before I ranged up alongside their right flank, and there was old Noscy, as we used to call Cardigan, well out to the front, and in front of him again was young Nolan of the 15th, with his sword down at the "right engage" already, although we were a long way off any enemy. Just as I came up in line with the flank sergeant of the front rank, who looked sideways at me as if I had been a ghost, Cardigan turned sound in his saddle to say a word to the field trumpeter riding at his heels, and then with a wave of his sword went off at score out to the front. In another second, all the trumpets of the brigade sounded the "charge," and sitting down on our saddles and setting our teeth hard, off we went pell-mell across the valley as hard as ever horse could lay foot to ground. Presently we got within range of the

devilish Russian battery which was playing right into
our teeth, and I saw Nolan, who was a long way out
to the front, galloping as if for a wager, toss up his
arms, and with a wild shriek fall from his horse. On
still, on we went, faster and faster as our horses got
excited and warmed to their work, heedless of the
torrent of shot that came tearing through us, and
stopping for ever many a bold rider. As for myself,
what with the drink in me, and the wild excitement
of the headlong charge, I went stark mad, and sent
the plucky Russian horse ahead at a pace which kept
me in line with the very foremost.

Nearer and nearer we came to the dreadful battery,
which kept vomiting death on us like a volcano, till I
seemed to feel on my cheek the hot air from the cannon's
mouth. At last we were on it. Half a dozen of us
leaped in among the guns at once, and I with one blow
of my axe brained a Russian gunner just as he was
clapping the linstock to the touch-hole of his piece.
With another I split open the head of an officer who
was trying to rally the artillery detachment in the rear ;
and then what of us were left went smack through
the stragglers, cutting and slashing like fiends, right
straight at the column of cavalry drawn up behind
the battery. What happened then, say you ? I
can't tell you much more than this, that they were
round us like a swarm of bees, and we, not more
seemingly than a couple of dozen of us to the fore,
were hacking and hewing away our hardest, each
individual man the centre of a separate *mêlée.* I
know I never troubled about guards myself, but kept
whirling the axe about me, every now and then
bringing it down to some purpose; and ever as it fell,

the Ruskies gave ground a bit, only to crush denser round me a minute after. Still nothing seemed to touch me. They dursn't come to close quarters with the sword, for the axe had a devil of a long reach ; and they dursn't use pistols, for they were too thick themselves.

I'm hanged if I don't half think I should have been there till now, had I not chanced to hear above the din a trumpet from somewhere far in the rear sound "Threes about." Round I wheeled, still thrashing about me like a windmill, slap through the heart of the battery again, knocking over an artilleryman or two as I passed, and presently overtook a small batch of men of various regiments, who, under Colonel Sewell of the 8th Hussars, were trying to retreat in some kind of order. I was as sober as a bishop by this time, take my word for it, and I joined them right cheerfully ; but the chances of getting back again to our own side of the valley looked very blue. The Russian cavalry were hard on our heels, and we suffered sorely from the devilish battery in our rear, which kept pelting into the thick of us, without much discrimination between friend and foe. The guns on those forts on our left, out of which the cowardly Turks had sneaked, and which had been pounced upon by the Russians, were not doing us much good neither, I assure you, and it was for all the world like being between the devil and the deep sea. Soon what little formation we had got was knocked to pieces, and then the word was, "Every man for himself, and God help the hindmost." A young fellow of the 11th Hussars and myself hung together for a while, both of us trying to make the most of our blown and jaded horses; but at last down he went, his horse shot under him, and himself wounded.   As the lad's busby rolled off when his head touched the ground, he gave a look up at me which went to my heart, rough as I was.   God pity him, he was little more than a boy, and I had a mother myself once.   I was out of the saddle in a twinkling, and had him across the holsters and myself in the seat again only just in time, for the damnable Cossacks were down upon us like so many wolves.   Oh! he was a good plucked one, was that little Russian horse ; right gamely did he struggle with the double load on his back, and hurrah! here were the heavies at last, and we were safe.

As I was riding to the rear to give the wounded man up to the doctor, I passed close under the staff, who were on the brow of the hill above me, but there was no notice taken of me that I perceived.   I rode up to our own camp, and by and by a sergeant came and made a prisoner of me, for the crime of breaking out of the guard tent when confined thereto—a serious military offence, I can tell you.   I wasn't shot for it, though ; for next day I was brought in front of Lord Lucan, who was in command of the cavalry, and who told me, that although he had a good mind to try me by court-martial, as, he said, I certainly deserved, he would let me off this time, in consideration of the use I had made of the liberty I had taken, and perhaps he would do more for me if I kept sober.   And that's how, sir, I came by this little medal, which is Britain's reward for distinguished conduct in the field.   Thank you, sir, I'll be sure to drink your health.

BUMMAREES.

H

BUMMAREES.

THE title of this article will, doubtless, form more or less of an enigma to the vast majority of readers. The origin of the name is involved in deep mystery. Who the first Bummaree was I am not in a position to state; but he has left a goodly progeny behind, not one of whom, however, so far as I am aware, is able to throw any light on the circumstances from which his peculiar name is derived. We are left, therefore, simply to accept the Bummarees as established facts, and, antiquarian research on the subject of their appellation failing us, to look at them as they are—links in the chain through which London is supplied. with an all-important article of consumption.

The Bummaree is not widely and casually diffused over the metropolis. Indeed, the fraternity are all concentrated in one locality, and that locality is not one affected from special choice by any great proportion of the reading population of London. Nor is he, even there, visible to the naked eye at whatever hour of the day we may choose to go in search of him. In fact, he has left the scene before many of us have finished our matitudinal tea and toast, and long before noon he has vanished for the day, and left not a trace

115

behind. If we want to see him in all his glory, a task
of no ordinary magnitude is before us—a task only to
be accomplished by a stern resolve, and prefaced by
portentous yawns and elaborate gymnastic feats in
the way of stretching.   Four o'clock in the morning
must see us out of bed, and on the way to study this
variety of the human species.   One word of caution
is necessary before leaving home.   It will be prudent
in more than one sense that we put on the very worst
garments our wardrobes can furnish.   Special precaution is needful in the article of head-covering.
The conventional tile must be abjured peremptorily
for various cogent reasons, which will appear here-
after, and a cap of the most tight-fitting—not to say
skull-cap—pattern will be found the most correct and
comfortable wear under the circumstances.   Thin
boots, too, are promptly to be repudiated.   A pair of
long thigh boots, if we have them, will stand us in
excellent stead, in default whereof our thick pair
of ankle-boots, surmounted by a pair of leather
knickerbockers, will tend materially to comfort and
cleanliness.

   Billingsgate Market is the theatre of our observation of the Bummaree. Arriving here about half-past
four o'clock we find it just awakening into full life.
The approaches to it are blocked half a mile each
way by railway vans piled high with fish-hampers
and salmon-boxes. Two or three smacks, uncountable
lighters, and a screw-steamer, are fast to the jetty,
and the market-porters are busily engaged in conveying into the market the fish with which they are
laden.   They deposit their burdens on and around
the various stands of the fish-auctioneers, who have

not yet commenced business, but whose men are in
attendance seeing to the correct disposal of the
various consignments.   Strange, amphibious-looking
people are dodging about in the open, unoccupied
spaces of the market without much apparent aim,
but soon we find them doff their coats, and having
seized on a coigne of 'vantage, proceed to erect a ram-
part of baskets round the position they have taken
up.   Suddenly a discordant bell rings out with a
harsh "cling, clang," the market is opened, and
everybody starts into activity, and becomes preter-
naturally wide awake.   Porters rush about frantically
with huge loads on their heads, and now you bless
your stars that your chimney-pot hat is on the hall-
table.   You are hustled on one side by a Colossus
with a salmon-box on his head, who imagines that the
magic words, " By your leave !" give him full licence
to butt you out of his path.   Getting out of his way
rather precipitately, you are brought up by an attack
of fish-baskets on the stomach ; an urchin with a
couple on his head is running amuck, and you are the
victim.   In much discomfiture you take refuge in a
comparatively quiet corner by one of the pillars, and
are congratulating yourself that you are out of harm's
way, when a sudden slam on the sloppy pavement
about an inch in front of you of a ponderous box,
accompanied with the warning shout of "Toes!"
rudely dispels this belief, and sends you backward
with an impetus which probably procures you a volley
of oaths both loud and deep from the lips of some
unfortunate you have cannoned against.   The auctioneers are by this time in their rostrums, selling
away with desperate rapidity and wonderful power of

lung. "Turbot! turbot! turbot!" is shouted in sten-
torian tones from one pulpit; loud roars of "Salmon!
salmon! salmon!" emanate from the opposite one;
the shouts of the auctioneer mingle with the responsive yells of the buyers; the din becomes positively
oppressive, and you feel you would give anything for
a moment's peace, but there is not even a second's
cessation.   The leathern-throated auctioneers bellow
louder, their men vie with them in the din, the buyers
get excited, and "bid out" vociferously, the rush of .
porters gets more bewildering, the general turmoil
and hurly-burly more wildly confusing.

I confess the likelihood is very strong, that after
having been jostled, trodden on, plentifully be-
sprinkled with fishy water, sworn at, chaffed, and
utterly deafened, you will be sorely tempted to scrape
the mud of Billingsgate from off your feet, and rush
impetuously from the scene of your tribulation up
one of the many narrow lanes which lead out of it.
But if you lose courage at this stage, and suffer yourself to be disheartened thus on the threshold, you
will lose your golden opportunity of making acquaintance with and studying the idiosyncracies of the
very men you are in search of—the Bummarees.
Wherefore, buffeted one, take heart and keep your
eyes open, and see what manner of men they are who
are thronging round the auctioneers' stands.

The contrast between the auctioneers and those who
surround them, you will observe, is very strongly
marked.   The former are sprightly, well-dressed, gen-
tlemanly-looking fellows, most of them gifted with
brazen throats surely, and with a volubility which
would almost put Mr Charles Matthews in the shade,

but evidently the patrons of fashionable tailors, not insensible to a weakness for well-fitting kid gloves, and displaying a *penchant* for the latest pattern in shirt-collars and the newest thing in neckties. The latter are of a different stamp altogether. They may be classed under three heads :— Rough—rougher—roughest. Great burly fellows the majority, with bluff faces, deep chests, and still deeper voices, with a smack of the waterman about them, a lingering suspicion of the costermonger as well, gruff and sparing of words, with eyes like a hawk's for a bargain, great unwashed fists, each one grasping a leathern money-bag, and with a faculty for mental arithmetic which is perfectly surprising.

These, good reader, are Bummarees and Bummarees' men. They fill an important niche in the economy of the fish-market. The leading fishmongers, who have a large demand for the different kinds of fish, no doubt, come in person or by deputy to the auctioneer's stand, and are purchasers at first hand of the large quantities they require to meet their extensive custom. But they are the exception. The great bulk of fishmongers and the whole fraternity of costermongers do not require fish in parcels so large as those sold by the auctioneers, and here the Bummaree steps in and makes his livelihood by acting as middleman between the large salesman and the retailer. He buys in the bulk from the auctioneer, and removing to his own " pitch" the fish so bought, he sorts it into convenient parcels, such as his experience tells him will meet the requirements of the class of customers he cares to attract. Of course he does not do this for nothing. Let us take the case of salmon, for instance.

The Bummaree buys half a dozen boxes from the auctioneer, sends them to his own pitch, and lots them out into various qualities and sizes according to the contents of each box.   The market price of salmon is fixed early in the morning by a sort of committee of the leading salesmen, and this the Bummaree pays to the auctioneer for his wholesale purchase.   He puts a price on his assorted goods sufficient to recoup him and leave a fair profit besides.   This profit in the case of salmon is a penny to three halfpence per pound, or as high as twopence if the customer makes but a small investment.   This increase in the cost the fishmongers find it their interest to submit to, and in preference deal with the Bummaree rather than with the auctioneer, because the latter sells in the pile and with all faults, so that the purchaser from him, in addition to having to make a large investment, has to take his purchase as it comes, good, bad, and indifferent altogether, when perhaps he has a market for only one quality.   The Bummaree, with one or another customer, has the means of disposing of all kinds ; therefore it suits his purpose to sort the large parcels, and he is accordingly patronised in preference by the retailer, whether he is a swell suburban fishmonger or a Whitechapel costermonger.   I say in preference ; but the truth is that a dealing with him, in many cases, is without choice, as when, from whatever cause—whether it be a limited requirement or a slender purse—a smaller purchase is desired than one of the large lots put up by the auctioneers.

A Bummaree, if he wants to live, must be a long way off a fool.   His judgment of fish in the bulk must be not only accurate, but has to be arrived at with a promptitude which, in the midst of the hurry-scurry of the market, and formed, as it apparently is, at little more than a simple glance, is something per-fectly wonderful to the uninitiated. Besides, he is, from the nature of his business, an habitual speculator. Fish is one of the few articles in which supply and demand do not bear a reliable relation to each other, and the Bummaree who buys incautiously may find himself at the close of the morning's transaction in danger of being left with a large unsaleable stock on his hands of a very perishable nature. Rather than do this, towards the close of the market he takes for his motto, " No reasonable offer refused," and then is the time for the wary and astute coster-monger who has studied the signs of the times to make a cent. per cent. bargain, long after his more impetu-ous fellows have supplied themselves at much higher rates or with other varieties, and are off on their rounds.

There are grades in this profession of the curious name. There is the swell Bummaree, whom you can hardly tell from the auctioneer (the aristocrat of the market), and who " bids out " freely for the choicest consignment of turbot and the highest-priced parcels of Tweed and Severn salmon, knowing that he will make his money out of the high-class West End fish-mongers, who *must* buy the pick of the market, no matter what the price may be. He doesn't trouble himself with the lower and cheaper classes of fish, but confines himself to the higher qualities, and the fish-mongers mostly clear him out by eight or half-past. The second-rate Bummaree, again, leaves alone stur-geon and turbot, and mullet and salmon, and goes in for soles, whitings, haddocks, and herrings.   His harvest is not over so early.   About eight o'clock there comes a fresh incursion into the market in the shape of small vendors, stall-keepers, and costermongers, rough of speech and gesture, full of strange oaths and practical jokes, "Hail fellow, well met!" with every one, in a rough-and-tumble, good-humoured, exuberant style of way ; and these are the chief customers of the second-rate Bummaree.   He doesn't do badly with them, although they are not so full of money as the swell fishmongers; but they are ready, eager buyers, and the class of fish they go in for is always in demand.

There is a casual Bummaree lower still in the scale.   He is a coster who has made a small pile, or perhaps he is a broken-down fishmonger who is turning his judgment to account.   Knowing the sort of fish likely to be most in demand, he throws in for a single lot (all he can afford) at the auctioneer's rostrum, and then removes his purchase to some pitch he has previously fixed on—perhaps had to fight for ; and having sorted it into the quantities he knows will suit the twopenny-halfpenny customers, who are all he can hope for, takes his chance of making a whacking profit out of them.   These casual Bummarees are principally found about the pillars supporting the water-front of the market, and are objects of the special vigilance of the market constable, who often, so fitful are the appearances of these worthies, finds it a matter of some difficulty to extract from them the market fee of sixpence, to which every one makes himself liable who takes up a pitch within the market boundaries.

A DESERTER'S STORY.

A DESERTER'S STORY.

I 'm a deserter, I am. But it's no use for the hateful man-catchers to think to collar me anywhere about London. They 'll never make a pound of blood-money out of my carcase, if I know it; for I 'm writing this by the light of a "Geordie," down in the depths of a coal-mine, and I daren't risk myself into the daylight, not even to put it into the post. I don't think the skulkers have pluck enough to come down here after me, but if they do they 'll go back empty-handed, if my right hand don't fail me. I 've sworn a bitter oath—and I 'm just the reckless outcast man to keep an oath of the sort—that I 'll never be took alive. I know too well what my fate would be, and I 'd sooner toil on here in the bowels of the earth, and never see daylight again while I have life, than I 'd be took back to the regiment, to be spread-eagled on the triangles, to have the cursed cat have its villain-ous will of me.

You 'll tell me, perhaps, I 'm like a wild beast down here, liker a mad savage than a man who was once a credit to himself and his belongings. So I am—I can't deny it ; but what made me so? What has brought me to this pass, that I am an outcast

125

from my fellow-men, afraid of my own shadow, a disgrace to kith and kin—a man who many a time don't care the toss of a farthing whether he be alive or dead to-morrow? If you think it worth your while to listen to me, I'll tell you, and then I would ask you to judge between me and my destroyers at whose door lies the blame in this matter.

Some six years ago there wasn't, though I say it myself, a smarter chap in all Yorkshire. An old chum, who had enlisted a few years before, came home on furlough one winter, and his talk set me a-thinking on going for a dragoon. Mind you, I didn't take the shilling in any crazy mood; but thought over the matter long before I made my mind up. I spoke about my notion to an old pensioner, who lived in our village, and his advice was "Don't;' and I wish to God now I had been ruled by him. But I wasn't, and so I went to the nearest recruiting-station, and took service in a cavalry regiment. In a week's time I was sent to headquarters, and before long I was in the riding-school all the morning and at foot drill all the afternoon. I won't say I wasn't a bit disappointed with the reality, when I came to experience it thoroughly, for the life wasn't altogether what I had put it down in my own mind, but still I wasn't unhappy, and the longer I was a soldier the more contented I grew. At length, by the time I was dismissed recruits' drill, I was as happy as a sand-boy. I knew my work, and could do it like a man; I was as fond of my horse as many a chap is of his brother; I was well-liked by my comrades, and my officers, if they didn't trouble their heads much about me, had at least nothing to say against me, for there wasn't so much as the scratch of a pen opposite my name in the defaulters' book. I was hardly scholar enough for promotion just then, but I was attending the regimental school every night, and I believed myself, and so did my mates, that before many months I should have the corporal's stripes on my arm.

I had been joined about eighteen months when a chap, whose real name I won't mention, but who used to go by the nickname of " Picco," was transferred into our troop out of another. He was a good soldier and a smart chap enough, but a bullying, overbearing fellow as ever I came across. He hadn't been in our room two days before he tried on his bounce, giving a white-faced slip of a recruit a slap across the mouth because he grumbled at the unfair way Picco was cutting out the messes of meat at dinner-time. The lad was my own chum, and I stood up for him, because he couldn't take his own part. In two minutes more Picco and I were at it in the riding-school, hammer and tongs, and in about ten I had given him as tidy a tying-up as he had got for many a day. It was the worst ten minutes' work I ever did myself, as you will presently hear.

In about another fortnight Picco was read out corporal. The stripes hadn't been on his arm two days when he began to show the cloven hoof, and to let me know that he meant, now he was up in the stirrups, to serve me out for the hiding I had given him when we were both privates. His commencement was to order me to fetch forage out of my turn to save a chum of his own, and when I asked him why he threw the duty on me, he swore he would put

me in the guard-room for insolence, if I so much as
dared to open my mouth. From this day he commenced a regular system of annoyance and oppres-
sion, directed against me with a cool deliberate
malevolence which was downright fiendish. Once or
twice he got me into trouble when he was corporal,
but his opportunities for doing me mischief were not
so great till he got the third stripe as sergeant. Then
his chances were increased an hundredfold, and there's
no mistake he never missed one. It was all one how
much I tried, I could never do a stroke of good. Day
after day he used to swear my saddle was put up
without being properly cleaned, although every man
in the stable knew I would no more think of setting
it on the peg dirty than I would of borrowing half-a-
crown off the colonel. I never could contrive to
clean old "Turk" to this man's satisfaction, and
he used to keep me grooming at him an hour
after the other chaps had gone up to dinner. My
kit on the shelf above my cot, and the arrangement
of my bedding, were always faulty according to his
showing, and it was his regular practice to order me
up from the stable in the middle of the mid-day
bustle to put them straight. It was no good for me
to protest that everything was in order, because the
cunning dog always took the precaution of pulling
the lot down in a heap on the floor beforehand ; so I
had not the ghost of a chance to impugn his word.
I never was out of hot water. I used to be up in
front of the captain day after day for complaints at
his instance, and was always getting three days' punishment drill. The captain used to shake his head,
and wonder what had come to me, who used to be so

clean and steady; but he never would give me the
chance to get a word in edgeways, to tell him that all
was owing to the sergeant's wanton malevolence. I
once formed up to him to make a formal complaint
that the man had his "knife into me," but it was no
good; he told me he was bound to believe and support his non-commissioned officer, and gave me to
understand that it would be worse for me if I ventured to make any representations of the kind again.

After this I began to get reckless, and if I had bitten
my tongue off, I couldn't refrain from opening out
and giving the fellow a bit of my mind, when I saw
how determined he was to keep chasing me. Just
what he wanted this—and I found myself between
a file of men in a twinkling, on my way to the guard-
room. There was never anything in the colonel's
mouth for a poor devil less than ten days' pack-drill
when a non-commissioned officer bore testimony
against him of "insolence;" and so it came to be that
I was hardly ever out of the barrack square; tramping
up and down, hour after hour, with my heavy kit on
my back, and bitterly cursing Sergeant Picco in my
heart. I knew the villain's game by this time—he
would fain have irritated me into striking him, with
his cool, vicious malevolence; and I swore to myself,
if he ever did aggravate me to this pitch, I would put
a mark on him he never would get rid of.

This persecution went on systematically for more
than a year. I had got seven days' cells (which lost
me my hair), my character was clean gone; and every
officer in the regiment, from the colonel down to the
sergeant-major of my own troop—a weak man, quite
under the thumb of my enemy—looked upon me as

I

a dangerous, ill-conditioned, mutinous dog. And yet there was not a single crime recorded against me but where this non-commissioned officer was my accuser; and it used to make me so wild, lying brooding in my cot of a night, that do what I could, I was utterly unable to convince my superiors that I was being slowly ruined through his persistent ill-will. But the more I tried to do so, the worse plight I always found myself in. I got put down as a "lawyer," the worst character the private soldier can possibly bear with his officers. At length the colonel told me once, when I was confined for the same eternal crime of "insolence" to Picco, that the next time I came before him, he'd send me for a district court-martial as sure as I was in life.

About this time I was taken ill, and had to go into hospital. I never was a skulker; and no sooner did I feel myself able to tackle the horse-brush and curry-comb again, than I asked the doctor's permission to return to duty. He granted it, but gave me strict injunctions to be careful of cold about the throat. Now, I had no neckerchief, and with the utmost innocence I asked one of the hospital orderlies to lend me one of those served out to the patients which I promised to return in a few days, when my throat got sound. This miserable kerchief came very near being the means of getting me flogged, as you will hear. A day or two after leaving hospital, before going down to mid-day stables, I took it off my neck, and stowed it inside my folded-up palliasse in the barrack-room. I was grooming away full steam when my foe came into the stable, and stopped at the foot of my stall as was his wont, casting about for some-

thing to find fault with.   Sharply calling me from my
horse's head, he asked me whether that wasn't my
bed which had the end of a kerchief sticking out of
its side.   Without a suspicion of evil, but thinking he
meant to be down on me for untidiness, I told him it
was, and said I'd go up at once and put everything
straight.   Stopping me as I went, he asked where I
had got the kerchief, to which I replied, still as innocent as you please, that I had borrowed it from hospital to put round my throat at nights.   Before I
could catch my wind I was under escort on my way
to the guard-room, to answer the charge of theft of
Government property.   The idea seemed to me
utterly ridiculous, for I made sure the orderly would
prove the fact that I had borrowed it from him.   But
I was mistaken.   He, it seems, had no right to grant
the loan, and so, to save his own bacon in the pinch,
he denied the conversation altogether.   It was in vain
I pleaded I had never attempted any concealment of
the worthless article, and that the idea of theft never
once entered my head.   I could see Picco had fairly
got me this time, and with my bad character, the skin
of my back was not worth an orange peel.

I got out of this scrape, however, by paying my
gentleman back in a little of his own coin.   A young
fellow, who knew all the circumstances, and had been
an attorney's clerk before he took the shilling, came
down to me in the afternoon into the guard-room,
and put me on a scheme to save myself.   I put it in
practice next day, when I went before the colonel
again to be formally committed for trial.   He briefly
recapitulated the facts, stating that I had been found
in unlawful possession of an hospital neckerchief, and

that he must send me for trial by a court-martial for
the disgraceful crime of theft. Now for my friend's
wrinkle. "Beg your pardon, sir," said I, "but I don't
understand you. I deny that I ever saw the kerchief
till the sergeant came into the stable. I don't admit
that it was in my possession at all. He says he
found it in my bed. He may have done so, or may
not. I utterly deny any knowledge of the article
whatever." "Why, you rascal!" roared the colonel,
"you confessed yesterday to bringing it out of the
hospital, and acknowledged to the sergeant it was
yours." "I retract the confession," I replied, very
demurely; "and besides, before a court-martial a
man's own confession is not admissible, and you must
prove the charge even if he pleads guilty." They
were all dumbfoundered in the lump. I was taken
back to the guard-room, and presently sent for again
into the orderly-room, after the consultation was
over, when the colonel called me "a —— lawyer," and
gave me ten days' pack-drill "on suspicion."

After this Picco never left me, and very soon he
got me a court-martial and forty-two days' imprisonment for "insubordination." When I was in the
prison, it was a good job for me, and for him too, that
we were kept apart; for when I brooded over the
long tract of systematic tyranny which had brought
me to this, there was many a time I worked myself
up to that pitch I could have killed him with as little
compunction as I would have crushed a horse-fly.
The sixth commandment was a dead letter with me,
so far as regards the "thought" part of it; and now
and then I found myself drifting into the deliberate
cogitation of schemes for summary vengeance as soon

as I should regain my liberty. I was, in fact, mad with the madness of despair; mad for that it was permitted that one man, because he had three stripes on his arm, should have the power, unchallenged, to work his malevolent will on an inoffensive fellow-soldier; mad that such a man should be able to blight and ruin a well-intentioned career. At this point my madness assumed a method, and I asked myself whether I was bound to a service whose regulations allowed of me being so maltreated? whether the grossness of my injuries did not assoilzie me from the oath I had taken on enlistment. You could hardly expect very rigid logic from a man who could point to wrongs such as mine; and, in short, I determined to desert the moment my hair had grown, and to leave mine enemy a mark to remember me by before I went.

It was some time before an opportunity occurred; but at last it did come. A man was "absent," and a picket had to be sent out after him. Picco was the non-commissioned officer, and I was the private whose turn it was for this duty. Through all the low beer-houses and all the soldiers' haunts we searched to no purpose. I was pretty well in funds, and the sergeant was short. I spent freely, and he drank as freely, and when he began to get a little warm I plied him with different mixtures till he was quite drunk. Then I took him out to the back court of the public-house, and told him to do what he could to take care of himself. To do him justice he was no coward, and he stood up to me like a man; but if he had been as sober as a bishop, and as scientific as Tom Sayers, I felt that in me which told me I must have had the best of it.

We weren't at it five minutes. At the end of that time, I brought him out into the street, bundled him inside a cab, and paid the driver to set him in the middle of the barrack-square. I knew his court-martial was a certainty. By nightfall I was a hundred miles away.

Now, my object in penning these rough lines is this. Don't, when you see a poor devil marched past you with the darbies on and a file of men with fixed bayonets on either side of him—don't, I say, always shrug your shoulders and say, " There goes a Queen's hard bargain." If you were to get at the root of the truth, you might find that at least a proportion had been baited to ruin by the tyranny of non-commis-sioned officers. I say nothing against the superior officers, except that it might sometimes accord with their duty at least to hear both sides of a story before they condemn, instead of believing, in their easy, careless way, in the sergeant's infallibility.

LIONS AND LION TAMING.

LIONS AND LION-TAMING.

BY AN EX-LION-KING.

AND so the beasts have savaged poor Jack Macarthy at last, have they? I expected it would come some time, sir, as soon as I heard poor Jack had forgotten the way to keep his little finger down. It's the drink that plays the mischief with us fellows; and yet how is a man to keep off it? He may be as bold and as sober as he pleases, till he gets once torn, and then his nerve begins to fail—wouldn't yours, sir, if you had half the flesh peeled off your side, or the side of your head torn off?—and he must have something to "steady himself" before he goes in. One steadier brings more, and there are plenty of people always ready to treat the daring fellow that plays with the lions as if they were kittens; and so he gets reckless, lets the dangerous animal, on which if he were sober he would know he must always keep his eye, get dodging round behind him, or hits a beast in which he ought to know that a blow rouses the sleeping devil, or makes a stagger and goes down, and then they set upon him. Don't I know the whole game from beginning to end? Look here, sir, and here,

137

where the living flesh has been torn off me, till the
bare bone was visible! I'm an old man now, but my
hair was grey when I was comparatively young, and
it was going into the den as did it.

I was never meant for a lion-king, for I never had any
nerve to speak of, only I was a big broad-built man,
and the management fancied me for the job. Old
"Manchester Jack" had given notice, and there were
the lions, and nobody to do anything with them. I was
a bill-sticker out of work when Bromsgrove spoke·to
me about the job. Mary Anne was down with twins,
and s'help me, sir, if I had a way to get her a drop of
comfort. Rather than see her starve I took the billet; but there never was a day when the time came
for me to go in among the devils that I did not try a
rough bit of a prayer, for that seemed somehow, for
the first while, to drive away the nervousness. Then
I found brandy took the shine out of the prayer, leastways such a prayer as I knew how to come; and I
used always to have a tidy drop inside me before I
ventured in. I knew the risk of the brandy. Didn't
I get this tear down the left arm one evening when I
had taken so much that I could not see that old ——
of a lioness creeping round to my back? But I couldn't
help it, and that's all about it. I had the *delirium
tremens* once, and my blood runs cold when I think of
that time. Other chaps as have had the *deliriums*
have told me as how they saw serpents, and black
tadpoles, and comical little devils, squatting all about
them, and making mouths at 'em. As for me, I was
haunted by lions and tigers all the time. Sometimes
it was the Royal Bengal tiger a-standing just over my
throat, with that great paw on my chest, and his hot,

strong breath blowing into my throat fit to choke me. Fancy, after I got up again having to go into the den after such a spell as that ! And then there was the wife at home, believing every night that I would be brought out to her a mangled corpse.

I don't say as all the lion-kings funk on it so bad as I did. Some of them has more nerve, and take to the work kindlier ; but there arn't ever a man going in the line as hasn't been torn or worried somehow since he began the game. Do I know the history of lion-taming, ask you ? I ought to. Having been in the profession so long, I know most of those who were comrades in it with me ; and then somehow I took a sort of morbid interest in hearing all the stories about tearing, and pluck, and what not, that might escape men who had less on their minds on the subject than I had. There are three kinds of lions come to this country. The greater number are fetched from the Cape ; some come from Egypt, but are really Nubian lions, and they are the biggest and dangerousest ; and another kind, the maneless sort, comes from Senegal. The man that imports nearly all the lions into this country is Jamrach, down in Ratcliff Highway. He has his agents out abroad, and also buys from stewards and captains of ships who bring the animals home on spec, and he sells them to the menageries and the Zoological Gardens. You get them from him well-nigh as wild as the day they were caught, for I believe he never allows any of his men to go into the cages, and if he wants to shift them he places one cage alongside another and drives the beasts in by setting fire to the straw in the den he wants them to quit if no other way will do. But even with these precautions his men sometimes get torn ; I am told he had a man badly hurt a short time ago.

I reckon that at present there are about fifty lions altogether in England, but of these only a certain number have been imported. You see, they breed like cats—have a litter every eight months if you will let 'em—and three, four, five, or six at a litter. The confinement-bred lions seldom live very long, and are not to be compared for looks to the forest-bred beasts ; but of course they are cheaper, and that has of late hurt the foreign market.

The tigers come from India, and don't breed so free in captivity. The tiger is not so sullen in confinement, but he is more treacherous ; and when he once loses command of hisself, there is not a pin to choose between him and the lion. I think I would sooner on the whole have truck with the lion than the tiger. Some people will tell you that there is no vice about either. Then I ask them, How is it that men who have to do with 'em get so often torn ? It is very easy to say that they let their talons out sometimes unwittingly into a chap's flesh, and that if he has the presence of mind he will lift the paw and think nothing about it. But when you feel the claws going into the flesh, an inch and more, may I never if you can help dragging the limb away. Then the beast drags *his* way, and so you get torn and the blood comes, and the animal, partly through the sight of blood, partly through a feeling of desperation at knowing he has done wrong, lets go anyhow ; and the others in the cage with him catch the infection, and then you may say your prayers.

The dangerousest time, ordinarily, to interfere

with lions is when they are feeding, especially if they are gnawing a bone. It is pretty well certain death for a man to go without warning to an old lion or lioness, and try to drag a bone away from it. You may switch them away, but it is very dangerous. Crockett used to take the most liberties with lions feeding of any man I ever saw. Then there are seasons when, if there be a lioness in a cage, both she and the lions that are with her are well-nigh mad with savageness, and daren't be interfered with if a man values his life a button. True, tamers have to go among them then, else business would be at a standstill ; but the chap that does so takes his life in his hand. I fancy that had something to do with the death of poor Jack Macarthy. They ought to have had the irons then ; for, indeed, when lions are like this, is the only time I ever knew irons to be in the fire in case of accidents.

The lion-tamer likes to get his beasts as young as he can, because then they are more easily brought into order, although, no doubt, there are many instances where a full-grown forest lion has been trained to high perfection. Whatever is the reason, the forest lions are more intelligent and teachable than those bred in confinement. The lion-tamer begins by taking the feeding of them into his own hands, and so gets them to know him. He commences feeding them from the outside of the den, then ventures inside to one at a time, always carefully keeping his face to the animal, and avoiding any violence, which is a mistake whenever it can be avoided, as it rouses the dormant devil in the beasts. Getting to handle the lion, the tamer begins by stroking him down the back, gradually working up to the head, which he begins to scratch, and the lion, which, like the cat, likes friction, begins to rub his head against the hand. When this familiarity is well established, a board is handed in to the trainer, which he places across the den, and teaches the lion to jump over it, using a whip with a thong, but not for the purpose of punishment. Gradually this board is heightened, the lion jumping over it at every stage ; and then come the hoops, &c., held on top of the board to quicken the beast's understanding. To teach the animal to jump over the trainer, the latter stoops alongside the board, so that when the lion clears one he clears the other; and half a dozen lessons are ordinarily about sufficient to teach this.

To get a lion to lie down and allow the tamer to stand on him is more difficult. It is done by flicking the beast over the back with a small "tickling" whip, and at the same time pressing him down with one hand. By raising his head and taking hold of the nostril with the right hand, and the under lip and lower jaw with the left, the lion, by this pressure on the nostril and lip, loses greatly the power of his jaws, so that a man can pull them open and put his head inside the beast's mouth, the feat with which Van Amburg's name was so much associated. The only danger is lest the animal should raise one of his fore-paws and stick his talons in ; and if he does, the tamer must stand fast for his life till he has shifted the paw. Lion-hunting, for which Maccomo was so famous, is never to be attempted except with young animals. When the lion begins to get his mane, and becomes near full grown, he will not suffer himself to

be so driven and bustled about ; and so it is that the
animals that are put through this performance are so
often changed. But most men with strong nerves
and high courage like an old lion best for ordinary
performances. His training is sure to be better, and
they take their chance of the temper, that always
grows crustier with age. But there are comparatively few old lions in England. It takes a lion well
into ten years to come to his full growth ; and when
this is once attained, confinement seems to bear uncommon hard upon them.

Who was the first lion-king in this country ? Well,
sir, I can tell you all about them, and, in fact, the
whole story about menageries. The first great
menagerie proprietor I ever heard anything on was
old Wombwell, who was originally a shoemaker in
the Commercial Road, and who first travelled about
with a big serpent. Before ever Van Amburg was
heard on, old "Manchester Jack" was doing the lion-
king in one of Wombwell's travelling menageries, well
on to fifty year ago. The manager, I remember well
his name, was Bromsgrove. He was a better man,
was Manchester Jack, than Van Amburg ; they were
to have had a regular competition once at Southampton, and lots of money was betted over the matter ;
but before the time came the American funked on it,
and would not come on. Jack took to hotel-keeping
in Taunton, with Bromsgrove for head waiter, and
died within the last seven years. Van Amburg, after
having been killed on paper over and over again, his
back broken twice at least, and his head once swallowed
by a Royal Bengal tiger, died in his bed within the last
three years ; but he must have been fearfully scarred.

Some of the old menagerie stories are funny
enough, sir, although there is gruesomeness about
them all.   Long ago, two men called Gilbert and
Atkins had a joint menagerie; a lioness belonging
to which got loose on Salisbury Plain while the
caravans were halted at a public-house called the
" Pheasant." Springing out of the ditch, she seized by
the throat one of the leaders of the mail-coach, and
tore it very much before she let go her hold, after the
guard of the coach had fired a shot into her with his
pistol.   Two men—one named Multer, the other
Reader—went after her, and caught her cowering
under a granary raised from the ground on arches.
She was brought back, muzzled, and tied with ropes,
and the proprietors bought the coach-horse, and drew
great audiences in Salisbury to see the identical
beast as the savage brute had torn so badly.   Did
you ever hear of old Wallace's fight with the dogs?
George Wombwell was at very low water, and not
knowing how to get his head up again, he thought of
a fight between an old lion he had—called Wallace—
and a dozen of mastiff dogs. Wallace was as tame as
a sheep; I knew him well—I wish all lions were like
him.   The prices of admission ranged from a guinea
up to five guineas, and every seat was taken; and
had the menagerie been three times as large it would
have been full.   It was a queer go, and no mistake!
Sometimes the old lion would scratch a lump out of
a dog, and sometimes the dogs would make as if they
were going to worry the old lion, but neither side
showed any serious fight, and at length the patience
of the audience got exhausted, and they went away
in disgust.   George's excuse was, "We can't make

'em fight, can we, if they won't?" There was no getting over this, and George cleared over £2000 by the night's work.

In later times, Crockett made the greatest name for himself of any lion-tamer, not in England alone, but also in France, Germany, and America. I remember well the time when the six lions were loose at one time in Astley's, when old Batty had the place. The Sangers had sent the beasts up from Edmonton the night before. Nobody to this day knows for certain how they got out of their dens; but it was thought at the time that some of the grooms— with whom Batty never was popular, he used to fine them so mercilessly—had let them loose maliciously, that they might get at the horses. There they were, anyhow, loose and mad in the place, smelling the horses, and mad to get at them. They had already killed a man, and half eaten him, when Crockett arrived ; without halting for an instant, he dashed in among them single-handed, with only a switch in his hand, and I'm blest if he didn't manage to den them all single-handed. That was nerve for you. At that time Crockett never drank. Crockett's history was a strange one. His mother was the finest woman I ever saw. She was exhibited for twenty years as "Miss Cross, the Nottinghamshire Giantess." She stood six feet nine, and broad in proportion, with quite a beautiful face. His father was a musician, as used to play the key-bugle, and the pair made a good deal of money. The way Crockett came to be a lion-king was curious. He was a fine-looking, imposing man, a musician in Sangers' Circus, but with a bad chest, which playing affected. When Howes

K

and Cushing came over from America with their
circus about fifteen years ago, they proved to be too
many for the home circuses of the day, and, in search
of novelty, the Sangers determined to try performing
lions from a menagerie. Crockett, being a fine-looking man, was offered the billet to perform them.
Originally he was a man of no nerve for lion performing, or any other calling requiring determination ;
but after seeing two or three others go into the den
with impunity, he accepted the job, and followed the
profession to the day of his death.   Howes and
Cushing took him to America at £20 a week, to perform the animals they had bought from the Sangers ;
and, after being in the States for about two years, he
fell down dead as he was "going on" about mid-day,
between the dressing-room and the circus.   This was
at Chicago.   Crockett was born at Presteign, in
Radnorshire, and several times was severely torn
while performing lions.

You ask about Maccomo ?   I know all about him
too.   There were two Maccomos—one a duffer, the
other the genuine article.   Some twenty years ago,
George Hilton's menagerie was at Manchester Fair,
with "Kitty" Lee for manager, a brother of the Nel-
son Lee who died the other day.   "Kitty's" real
name was Jem, but everybody called him "Kitty."
Newsome, who was the performer of the lions, had
left without an hour's notice, and Lee was aground.
But a man named Jemmy Strand, who kept a gingerbread stand, came forward, and volunteered to perform them at a moment's notice, and Lee christened
him "Maccomo" on the spot.   Strand was an Irishman, like poor Macarthy ; and his head got so turned

by success, that nothing could be done with him, and his sauce was unbearable. One day at Greenwich Fair, a musician, playing in front of the menagerie, came to Mr Maunders, into whose hands Hilton's business had passed, and told him that there was a black man outside, who said he was a sailor just come home from sea, and would like to get a job with the wild beasts. Mr Maunders sent for him, struck a bargain, and sent him into the den at once, and the black man proved to have a wonderful control over the beasts, so that the "gingerbread king" lost his crown at once, and the black man got his name of Maccomo, which he bore till he died of consumption about fifteen months ago. Maccomo was the most daring man among lions and tigers I ever saw. At first he never drank anything stronger than coffee, but he always believed he would meet a violent death. He was fearfully torn over and over again, but not killed. It was riskier for him than for a white man, if it be true, as they say, that the beasts can nose a black man, and are mad after the flavour of his flesh.

These are about the leading lion-kings I remember, but there have been many others of less note. As a rule, drink is what plays the devil with them all, and you can hardly wonder at it. Ah! so you have heard about lion-queens too, have you? Well, I can tell you all about them also. The first lion-queen came out in Joe Hilton's circus, at the suggestion of "Kitty" Lee, to counterbalance the attraction of Crockett as a lion-king, and he proposed that Hilton's daughter should come out as the lion-queen, as she had previously been in the den with

the lion. He proposed that she should appear under
the name of " Madame Pauline de Vere, the Lady of
Lions," and so she did.   I remember her first appearance quite well.   It was at Stepney Fair; and didn't
she cut a dash on the platform in front of the menagerie before going into the den? At this time Mr
Wombwell's menagerie—as was under Edmonds'
management—had an excellent group of wild beasts,
and Miss Helen Chapman (now Mrs George Sanger)
volunteered to perform with them as the rival lion-
queen to Madame de Vere.   You may have heard of
Miss Chapman's appearance before the Court at
Windsor.   At another of Wombwell's menageries
another lion-queen came out soon after—Miss Helen
Blight; but she had not performed long before she
was killed by the tiger.   It was at Greenwich Fair,
and I was in the menagerie at the time. As Miss
Blight turned from one tiger—the oldest—to perform
the other, the old devil, with a roar and a lash of his
tail, sprang at her, got her by the throat, and she was
well-nigh dead before they got her out of the den.
After this horrible mischance, lion-queens were prohibited by order of the Lord Chamberlain; and a bad
day it was for the treasury, for they used to fetch the
money in better than anything else. But it was time.
Here was Helen Blight killed, and both Madame de
Vere—Polly Hilton as was—and Miss Chapman had
been badly torn more·than once.

Lions are just like human beings—every one has
got his temper. Some you might trust for ever till
they tasted blood; others you cannot watch too
cautiously, for they will pin you if they can. And
then in confinement, you see, they get used to the

human eye, and it ceases to work any effect upon
them. But the worst time for the performer is when
the lions and a lioness are together at the season I
have already spoken about. What a battle-royal
that was once at Weymouth among Sangers' lions!
There were five lions and a lioness. One of the lions
used to be brought out of a morning and driven in a
fancy car round the town, with a lady beside him,
the pair representing Britannia and the British lion.
One morning, when we came to take out this lion, we
found the den a pool of blood, and the lions fighting
furiously with each other, their manes up, their
talons out, and their eyes flashing. We all funked
on it, we lion-kings. There was Crockett, Bill
Phubbs, Billy Strand, "the gingerbread king,"
"Nosey Joe"—a well-known tamer, so called because his nose had been split right open by a blow
from a leopard's paw—and myself; and not one of
us would venture. But George Sanger did. Snatching the hand-whip, he jumped off the wheel of the
carriage into the den, shot in among the beasts, beat
the lions on one side, and the lioness on the other,
and made a barrier between of the boards that we
shoved in to him. Then Crockett got his nerve
again, and at the termination of the equestrian performance, he brought the five males into the ring,
and put them through their regular feats.

Why, it's not long ago since some lions were
nearly loose in Islington. Perhaps you have seen
"one-armed Reeves." Some few years ago he was
connected with a circus in the Agricultural Hall.
All of a sudden the cry arose, "The lions are loose!
the lions are loose!" and Reeves came rushing up

the corridor streaming with blood, and making wildly
for the street. Mr Layard, the under-secretary of
the hall, caught him, and laid him down on the floor,
bandaged the arm, and sent for the doctor. He
went into the hospital, where his arm had to be amputated, and all just because one of the lions suddenly
got hold of it as he was settling the straw by the door
of the den while he was unused to the beasts.

If you could stop long enough, sir, I could tell you
lots more about lion-taming and lion-tamers ; but you
say you must go. Well, in parting, let me tell you
that I think the wisest thing the Lord Chancellor
could do would be to abolish lion-kings as well as
lion-queens. They risk their lives several times a
day, and that for no useful object whatever.

CATS'-MEAT.

CATS'-MEAT.

MY friend was a good-looking, clean-shaved person, with a shiny hat, a good black coat, and a pair of kid gloves. His "good lady" accompanied him, a buxom matron, not such a very great way behind the fashion-books as regards the style of her costume, and there were two handsome tidy children snugly packed into a neat perambulator. The time was Sunday evening, and the scene Victoria Park, that lung of London so specially affected by East-enders in their best habiliments, else it would have taken a great deal to persuade me that it was not a case of mistaken identity. The man might have been a " Conservative working-man," or he might have been a compound householder, or, in fact, anything conveying a notion of intense respectability, so regardless of expense was the appearance made on the promenade by himself and family this summer afternoon. After all, though, I could hardly be mistaken in the smart, good-humoured, active, cats'-meat man whom I encountered on his round on a previous week day, and who, then refusing any parley whatever on any terms, by reason of the dislocation it would entail on his punctuality, hurriedly told me that he was a

153

constant Sunday-evening visitor to "the Park," and
that he was at my service whenever I might choose
to see him there. Notwithstanding I was pretty sure of
my man, it was with some diffidence that I addressed
him; but I am profoundly glad to be in a position to
record the fact that he wasn't at all proud, nor mercenary, nor a swiller of beer, for he repudiated with
something like indignation my suggestion that he
should accept some remuneration for his information,
and when he had summarily knocked this idea on the
head, and I had moved an amendment to my own
proviso, in the shape of an offer of unlimited beer,
my friend quietly remarked that he was "next door
to a teetotaller." So, having sent "missus and the
kids" up a little nearer the stand, to be in a good
place for hearing the band, we two sought a retired
seat, and my informant imparted to me the following
facts in as nearly as possible the following language :—

"Well, there's worse trades than meat, and there's
better. When it's cheap wholesale, and a man has a
good 'walk,' and a fair connection, a tidy penny can
be earned at it in a week, enough to keep a wife and
family comfortable, though it won't 'xactly run to
champagne and a carriage and pair. Still, it's an
independent life and an active life, and one always
knows that the harder he works the better he will be;
so you see there's some encouragement for working.
There's more than one quality of cats'-meat sold in
London; in fact, it varies full as much as butcher's
meat. Perhaps you would make a poor fist as a
judge of it, but we dealers are as particular when we are
layin' in our stock as if we were with the old woman
a-buyin' the Sunday's dinner. A great deal comes up

daily by train from Liverpool and Glasgow, and even over from Ireland, although you would hardly think it would cover the carriage. Some used even to come from France at one time; but since the natives there have took to eat their own cats'-meat, horse finds a much better market in Paris than in London, and I did hear some talk lately about exporting it. Give me good London-killed meat, though. It's true, it costs a few shillings a hundredweight more, but still it's cheaper; because, for one thing, you buy it direct of the slaughterman, and so there's no middle-man's profit. Besides, it's fresher, of a better nature, and will cut so as to give more satisfaction to the customer as well as the dealer, than the half-withered tack that's travelled two or three hundred miles. We've got, I think, six London slaughter-men that I know of, and most of them do a very good business, one or two being quite in a large way of trade. The biggest yard is up at Belleisle, on the north side of the town, but there are several close round the Mile End Gate, and, in fact, you may put Whitechapel down as the headquarters of the trade. The slaughtermen have large sheds, in which the meat is laid out to be retailed to the hawkers, and the cats'-meat market lasts from six to ten, the first-comers, of course, getting the pick of the quality. It is sold by the hundredweight, the half and quarter hundredweight, and some take as little as fourteen pounds; and perhaps you'll hardly believe me when I tell you what the price runs at.

"Well, it varies, and just now it's very dear, but if you like to come with me to-morrow morning to Barber's, I don't mind betting you a day's taking that you can't buy meat that any hawker with any self-respect would take about under 16s. or 17s. a hundredweight. I have known it even dearer than this, but still we reckon it a tight fit to do much good at such a price as that; for let the wholesale market fluctuate ever so much we can never alter our prices, and the ladies very soon begin to grumble at the small ha'porths if we try to dock it out of them in the way of quantity. We have just got to stand the racket when the wholesale price is high, and make up for it a bit in the winter-time when the figure is low, because the meat will keep longer. Country meat we can get as low as 12s. or 14s. a hundredweight, but it is principally the casuals who invest in this sort, for a hawker with a regular walk and good customers to please dursn't venture on the cheaper quality, because he knows it wouldn't give satisfaction.

" I don't wonder that you are a bit surprised at this price. But the fact is, horseflesh, live or dead, is rising every day, and we shall have to take to something else if they manage to coax Britons into eating horse; but that won't be to-morrow. Why, a good-sized horse in fair condition is worth to the knacker before he is slaughtered from £3, 10s. to £5, and off such a beast as this several hundredweight of meat will come, leaving him besides the hide, hoofs, bones, &c. The bones are all taken out before boiling, and so when the meat comes into the sheds to be sold to us hawkers, it is in great shapeless blocks, just as it comes out of the coppers. We call them 'joints,' although a butcher would laugh at the use of the word; and by far the best joint of the animal is the hind-quarter. You don't get all hind-quarter, though—never fear ; you are forced to take a part of your weight in rib pieces, legs, or heart. The offal is sold separately and much cheaper. It goes for dogs' meat.

" The stock-in-trade of us hawkers is not heavy. It consists of a pair of scales, a sharp knife, a basket, a bundle of wooden skewers, and a barrow. A cats'-meat man who respects himself and has a proper pride in his profession always lays himself out for as dandy a barrow as he can get hold of, and puts as much paint and ornamental carving on it as it will carry. I knew a man once who was three years making a barrow in his spare time, and when it was done he wouldn't have taken a £20 note for it.

"Some of us take the meat home and cut it up before we start on our round, but the most of us cut it up as we go on the board of our barrow. It's here where the great art of the clever cats'-meat man shows itself—to cut the meat so that each ha'porth looks bulky and good value, and at the same time make as many ha'porths out of the pound of meat as ever you can. You might think this an easy job enough, but I tell you you must serve a regular apprenticeship to the trade before you can cut meat in a workmanlike fashion. The best hand I ever saw in the trade—he could lick me all to pieces, and I'm not a duffer—is a chap who has been a Wauxhall waiter, and used to cut plates of ham once on board Gravesend boats. He'll sliver up a single pound so as to cover nearly a square yard, and somehow he has the art of beginning and leaving off thickish, so as to make the edges look respectable, and the centre of the cut is difficult to guage. How many ha'porths

go to a pound, you ask ?   You 'll excuse me, sir, but
every profession has its secrets, and though I 'm willing enough to be free with you, the line must be
drawn somewhere, and if you don't mind, sir, we 'll
draw it at this delicate point.   You may take your
oath of this, however, that we do the best we can for
ourselves in this way, and another thing, that the
public take precious good care it doesn't allow us to
do too well.   There are places here and there—such
as large warehouses, wharves, and the like—where
they take half a pound from us in the lump, and we
charge them at the rate of 2½d. per lb., weighing the
meat as we serve it.   This don't give a bad profit,
but there 's not enough of it ; and after all I 'd sooner
do business in ha'porths, for though you work harder
to sell them, you make a better profit out of them.

"Well, we mostly get started on our rounds by nine,
and working briskly, and not stopping to gossip, one
can get over a good walk by five.   If you have a boy
or a girl to carry the basket up the side streets, while
you are serving the main thoroughfares, you can get
along faster ; but the young 'uns, I find, often lose
you money through inattention, and forgetting where
they have given credit.   Credit do we give, say you ?
Ay, that we do, and must, if we would keep our
connection together; and it 's a true thing I say,
although not very creditable to London householders,
that we are often left in the hole over it.   My experience has convinced me that when a family which
is moving may be ashamed or afraid to leave tradesmen's bills unpaid, and such like, there are three folks
they hate paying like poison, when they can possibly
wriggle out of it, and these are the tax-gatherer, the

milkman, and the cats'-meat man. If there is the least touch of bad principle about the party, be sure he will try to slope them; and many's the time, through the help of the bobby on the beat, who takes stock of the van which moves them, that I have traced them, and made them book up—and silly enough they look, I tell you. I always mistrust a missus who lets her meat score run up to 3s. or 4s. just afore quarter-day. But still I have been owed as much as 15s., and been paid honourable; but it's the exception if you get it without a row after you let it get over the 5s.

Like every other trade a living can be squeezed out at, the cats'-meat profession is awful overdone, and no matter if you secure what you think a regular walk to yourself, and reckon yourself safe in it, you will find "poachers" knocking about it trying to undersell you, and taking your customers off you as don't know your face. This is what makes it so bad for you. If you are forced by reason of illness, we'll say, to be off your walk yourself for a week or so, and let anybody else work it for you, depend on it, when you get about again, you will find a lot of your customers collared, and told a pack of lies about you being in quod, and that the "poacher" has bought the goodwill of your connection off your "grass widow." Are there such things, ask you, as sales of walks, then? That there are; and a good walk is as marketable a thing as anything I know. Why, across in Waterloo Town, there is a chap who knocks out a very good living by acting as a cat's-meat walk broker. I wouldn't advise you, though, if you were after a walk, to have any truck with him. It's a chance if he don't find you a fellow as will sell

you a walk, draw your chips for it, and be poaching
on you as cool as winkin' in a fortnight's time.   The
plan is to get hold of some genuine cove, who has
saved a bit of money on a walk, and means going in
for something better.   For we 're an ambitious set,
we cats'-meat men, and just as they tell me a clever
actor is never satisfied till he gets ruined as a manager, so a nobby cats'-meat man is never easy till he
has bought a pony and a light cart, and then his next
look-out is for a shop, or mayhap a beerhouse.   That 's
the sort of chap to buy a right walk of; but you
musn't think he 'll let you have it for nothing.   Mine's
not a bad one, but I had to stump out thirty quid
down on the nail for it, and pay half of the lawyer
besides.   Not that I grumble though—it 's worth the
money to a man that knows how to keep the connection together.   There was a talk some two years ago
of a lot of City swells buying up the business of some
of the largest hawkers, and making a limited liability
company out of them, under the title of the Grand
Metropolitan Cats'-meat Hawking and Vending Company, but the coin was not forthcoming, and so the
thing fell through.   One of the largest slaughtermen,
though, has recently sold his business to a company
at a whacking price, something like ten thousand
pounds they tell me.

You ask me which parts of the town make the best
ground?   Now, it 's a strange thing, but the best parts
of the town for most purposes is the worst for ours.
The swell West-End streets would starve a cats'-meat
man, for the nobs keep their cats on chickens and
weal cutlets, and chuck grub into the swill-tub that
many a Christian in Whitechapel would be thankful

for. Commend me to a quiet little street in the suburbs, where the folks are pretty stationary, where the missuses answer the door themselves, and know your face, and are not above passing the goodwill of the morning ; and, above all, where there are a tidy proportion of old maids. They grumble, they do, sometimes of the meat, 'specially in the heat of summer time, but it 's always because of quality, not quantity ; so I always study the spinsters, and lots of them have a penn'orth regularly. The City 's a wonderful good spot—there 's plenty of warehouses, and cellars, and offices, and the housekeepers all keep cats for company's sake ; and, besides, there 's no fear of any of them running away for a bob's worth of cats'-meat. But the ground there is all in one man's hands, and a nobby thing he makes of it, I can tell you. He 's got a pony to help him in his round that can do anything but speak, and a little cart as dandy as a picture ; and the set of plated harness might do for the Lord Mayor himself. But, Lord bless you, he 's the swell of the profession. He does a hundredweight and a half a day, an' he 's got a semi-detached willa down at Hackney, an' a chap did tell me he saw him and his missus coming out of the Hitalian Hopera the other night. I don't mind one night a week at the Brit. or the Surrey myself, but the Hopera, I must allow, is a chalk above me jist at present.

You want some statistics about the trade, you say. Well, it 's a rum trade—profession 's the c'rect word —to make fixed calculations about, but I won't say that I haven't amused myself sometimes reckoning up some figures about it. It 's no easy job, by reason of the different parts of the town where the sheds are,

L

to come at anything for certain about the weight of
the meat consumed in London daily; but considering
everything, I reckon there's about twelve tons cut
up every morning. I have spoken to one or two
about it, and we all make it pretty close the same
figure. As I have told you, there are about two
hundred and fifty regular carriers at the game every
day, besides outsiders and poachers, and kids that help
their parents. Well, now, there's a question! How
many cats are there in London? Why don't you go
to some parliament-man, and ask him to move for a
return of the number of individuals of the feline
species in the metropolis? That's the proper full-
mouthed way of putting it, isn't it? Still I think if
I were to try, I might get at the number of rations
of cats'-meat that are dispensed every day, and that
would at least give you the number of legitimate cats
kept in a proper and Christian manner. Suppose I
put you up to something, after all, and tell you a
pound of meat ought to cut into seven ha'porths.
Well, allowing that I sell half a hundredweight, that
will give about four hundred cats that I provision in
the day, and reckoning, as I have said, that twelve
tons go out, that won't give you far short of two hundred thousand cats eating cats'-meat daily in London.
Perhaps you may think my figures are a little over
the mark, guv'nor, but I don't believe, after all, you
will find me far out. And now I see the missus is
getting impatient, for it's near the young uns' bed-
time, and so I will say good-night. If you've a mind
to go round the walk with me any day, you're heartily
welcome, and you'll have a very good chance of
studying human nature in a new light.

ARMY CRIMES AND PUNISHMENTS.

ARMY CRIMES AND PUNISHMENTS.

AT a meeting once, of cab-drivers, in Exeter Hall, a certain quaint worthy of that fraternity, who proclaimed his name to be Tommy Toolittle, made the assertion that it was possible for a cab-driver, in the course of a single drive, to incur fifty pounds' worth of fines, as the accumulated penalties for possible breaches of the multifarious Cab Acts. Tommy seemed to think the Cab Laws constituted the most Draconian code sanctioned by our Legislature ; but then Tommy, judging from his size (to which his name was an index) could never have been in a position to accept the Queen's shilling, as tendered at the hand of a recruiting-sergeant, and therefore was not likely to be acquainted with the provisions of the Mutiny Act. Under the unrepealed clauses of it— obsolete possibly, but still valid—the punishment of " death or such other sentence as a court-martial may inflict" is still kept suspended over the soldier as the penalty for sundry offences, which the civilian could hardly consider to merit· so severe an expiation. True, this severity exists only *in posse*, and we owe it probably quite as much to the influence of public opinion as to the humanity of the powers that be of our military system that the alternative permitted in the above quotation is always had resort to. Nor is it possibly injudicious, with a far-sighted regard to the possible requirements of discipline during war time in a foreign country, that the power of enforcement of the sterner alternative as an ultimate resort has not been abrogated. What I am now desirous of doing is not to adduce examples of the operation of the army penal code, with the purpose of illustrating its abstract severity, but merely to narrate a few anecdotes, bringing out in some measure the comical side of the question, and illustrative of curious punishments for extraordinary and out-of-the way offences.

His own experience, with every man who has served in the ranks, will contain for certain not a few reminiscences of this nature ; but before giving any instances having reference to our own times, I do not think that some recollections furnished to me by an old pensioner will be destitute of interest. The old man is still alive. He served the Queen in every quarter of the globe during a period of forty years, commencing in 1800, when, as yet, the fathers of the current generation had hardly been thought of, and he is still a hale and hearty old fellow, who can relish a moderate tot of brandy as well as he did sixty years ago. One of his yarns I give nearly in his own words :—

"It was in the winter of 1812. The ould corps was taking part in the campaign against the Amerikins, and Sir George Prevost was commander-in-chief. We were laying in the fort of York in Upper Canada (now Toronto). Some of the chaps had been down in the settlement, and had got a tolerable skinful of Canadian whisky. One of them was a chum of my own—a man who had enlisted under the Seven Years' Act. His time was up, but he hadn't been discharged

because we were in front of the inimy. Well, the
party were returning to the fort at night, and this
chap, foolish-like, up with his stick and knocked
down a duck that was waddling on the roadside.
The ould Canadian that owned the duck followed
him up into the fort and made a report to the officer
on duty.   Bedad, Bill was shoved into the guard-room,
tried by a general court-martial, and what d'ye think
he got?   Only 999 lashes.   Aye, and he took them
all at one dose one frosty morning, when your spittle
would freeze before it got to the ground—and he
never said Bo! but just put on his coat and walked up
to the hospital.   And, what was better still, the chap
got his discharge and came home to England, and
the regiment followed soon after—and be hanged if he
didn't 'list again for the self-same corps in which he had
got 1000 lashes save one for knocking down a duck that
he hadn't even the satisfaction of picking up."

My pensioner friend is very garrulous about a certain old chum of his named Johnny Reilly, who had
received so many lashes at different times he had lost
all count of them.   At a certain mess-dinner, one
officer made a bet with another that Johnny had in
his time received over 3000 lashes.   Johnny was
appealed to, and after much harking back to old
flogging bouts, and great exercitation of spirit, de-
clared his utter inability to give satisfactory information on the point.   The books of the regiment were
referred to, and in them stood considerably over the
3000 lashes down to Johnny's account since his transfer from another regiment in which he had formerly
served.   When this piece of information was communicated to Johnny, he quietly remarked, without
taking the pipe out of his mouth, " For once I have

been flogged in this corps, I was twice touched over
in the ould one." This, if true, would give a wonderful sum total of lashes Johnny had received in his
time. His back had got nicely calloused, my friend
naively remarked, and he would take his 300 of a
morning nearly as much as a matter of course as he
would his breakfast. And yet Johnny was not a bad
soldier, it appears, and duly earned his pension.
Absence for a night brought 300 down on a fellow's
back in those days ; one of Johnny's doses of 300 was
for being drunk while cooking for the company. As for
pack-drill, in those days "you got it for luikin' cruickit."

I confess there is not a great deal of the comic
element in the infliction of a thousand lashes for the
high crime and misdemeanour of knocking down a
duck. And although there is something very humili-
ating in the fact, that, within the present century, a
British soldier should have been flogged till he had
lost his reckoning, one can hardly help laughing at
Johnny Reilly's imperturbable nonchalance on the
matter of a few hundred lashes more or less. In these
latter days, happily, there are no such repulsive ingredients in a story or two which occur to me, the
circumstances of which happened under my own
observation.

In a certain barrack-yard a squadron of dragoons
were drawn up on foot parade, and were being inspected by an officer who had lately joined the
regiment, and was afflicted with an insurmountable
stutter. On his way down the ranks he halted in
front of a soldier, whose appearance did not please
his eye. "Your b-b-belts are v-v-very d-d-dirty, sir,"
was his criticism. "I b-b-beg your p-p-pardon, sur,"
remonstrated the private, "but the p-p-pipeclay

wos very b-b-bad." The officer's face flushed scarlet in a minute, as a titter ran along the ranks, "Cuck-cuck-confound you, sir, are you mocking me?" "N-n-no, sur," replied Jack, "by no m-m-manes." "D-d-damn your impudence," roared the officer, "p-p-put him in the g-g-guard-room, sergeant." And so the private was marched off parade, stuttering most vehemently as he went, and the more he laboured to explain the angrier grew the officer. The crime went in against him of "insolence to an officer on parade," and when he appeared before the commanding officer next morning, being mortally afraid of opening his mouth at all, for fear more stuttering would be construed into more insolence, he was complimented with seven days' pack drill. I am not aware that this had the magical effect of loosening the knots in his tongue, but I believe he took exemplary care never to open his mouth again in reply to an officer on any consideration whatsoever.

The great "hair" question is one which has long proved a fertile source of discontent and grumbling in the army. In the old days of queues and powder and pomatum, many a soldier, I doubt not, regretted that he had not been born, if not without a head, at least without any hair upon it. Now-a-days in regiments where the regulation length, or rather shortness, is rigidly enforced, there is a chronic feud between the regimental barber and the young dandies who are given to curls and lovelocks, with which cherished ornaments his ruthless shears materially interfere. The facial hirsute appendages have likewise caused no end of heartburnings. Before the Crimean war it will be recollected that infantry regiments were not allowed to wear moustaches. On

the other hand, cavalry soldiers were compelled to
sport them, or the semblance of them. We have
never heard that a bottle of "thine incomparable oil,
Macassar!" or of Miss Skene's Grinoutriar was served
out to the smooth-faced recruit as part of his kit, and
that he was sequestered from the public eye till those
specifics had taken effect; but every old dragoon
will remember how the young fellows whose upper
lips were not clad with the virile token used to
blacken the bottom of a plate over a lamp or candle,
and with the colouring matter produced by this process improvise a pair of moustaches before going on
parade. A pair of "real false" ones used to circulate
through a troop for guard-mounting occasions, and
bring in a nice little royalty to the fortunate possessor. The whiskers in those days were cut with
mathematic precision, a nearer approach to the corner
of the mouth than two inches being rigorously forbidden, and indeed the approved pattern was of the
sternly mutton-chop character. Since the Crimean
war, however, the tendency has been to much greater
latitude, and a soldier's face may now be a perfect
thicket of hair, provided he reserves on the chin a
space of three fingers' breadth subject to the do-
minion of the razor. In some regiments, particularly
in cavalry ones, the profuse growth of hair on the
face is encouraged, as calculated to give the soldier a
martial look, especially if a helmet or a bearskin be the
head-dress. And perhaps nowhere is the custom of
dying whiskers (technically burking) so common as in
in the ranks of the army, where a deep black, quite
irrespective of the colour of the hair, is the recognised
standard hue of whiskers and moustache. To return
from this diversion, which, however, has a purpose.

In a certain cavalry regiment, the members of which prided themselves highly on their hirsute and fierce appearance, there was a dragoon whose facial adornments in the way of hair were splendid. He cultivated them with much pains, and was always selected for any duty where there was a chance of a comparison being instituted between him and the picked men of other corps. On one occasion this hirsute individual was showing a saddle belonging to another man, and its condition brought down the wrath of the inspecting officer, and a peremptory order to clean it thoroughly. Not being responsible for the condition of the saddle, the man was much hurt at the slur on his soldierly qualifications. He made no remonstrance, however, did as he was told, walked quietly up to his barrack room, took out his razor, and cut—well, not his throat—but his whiskers and moustache clean off. At next parade he appeared with a face as smooth as an apple, and was at once made a prisoner of. When he came before the commanding officer, that dignitary's wrath was unbounded. To mitigate the same, the man attempted a plausible excuse to the effect that he had been " burking," and that one whisker had come out green, the other blue—an anomaly which had prompted him to remove them altogether ; but the explanation, smacking as it did of a bouncer, did not placate the angry colonel, who proceeded to inflict sentence. This comprised, of course, the inevitable seven days' pack drill, in addition to which the man was ordered to be confined to barracks till his hair was grown. The sentence was rigidly enforced. Every now and then the fellow would piteously form up to the adjutant, and entreat that he should be certified as decent ; but this devoutly-wished-for consummation was not achieved till he had been inside the barrack gate for three months. Long before then he was heartily sorry that he had made so free with his razor. The strict law on the subject is, I believe, that a soldier's whiskers are his own—that is, if his regiment has not a vested interest in them ; but that his moustache belongs to the Queen, and to shave it off is just in effect as bad as if he were to make away with any of his other necessaries.

A general was, some years ago, making the annual inspection of a regiment of foot-guards. The men had been on parade all the morning, and when it was over they returned to the barracks as hungry as wolves. The dinners were brought from the cook-houses and divided, and the men only waited for the formal visit of the inspecting general to fall to and eat. The bugles sounded " Dinner up," but still he came not. For a stricken hour did he stand chatting in the barrack square with the regimental officers, under the noses of the hungry men, the dinners meanwhile growing colder and colder. At last he commenced his tour of inspection, heralded by bawling non-commissioned officers, and accompanied by the smirking staff. In each room he put the usual question—" Any complaints ? "—and met with none till a savage private replied, " Yes, sir, I report my messing cold." The great man glowered on the presumptuous private for some moments without speaking ; at length he broke silence with the blandly-uttered words, " That is my fault, my man ; " and then, turning to the commanding officer, finished his sentence with—" Colonel, let that man have ten days' pack drill."

THE STORY OF THE *MEGÆRA*.

THE STORY OF THE MEGÆRA.

"THE *Pera* telegraphed?" "No, sir, she's about due at five this afternoon"—the place was Southampton, and the day the Saturday on which the first batch of the *Megæra's* were expected to reach England—"but the wind is dead against her up channel, and she's not a specially quick boat." Five o'clock came, and no *Pera*. Ten o'clock came, and still no *Pera*. But the big ship had been telegraphed from Hurst, and about ten the mail-boat was going out to her. Would it be wise to go with the mail boat? It was not certain but that the *Pera*, declining to be interviewed by the little craft, would come right into dock before she stopped, and so give one the go-by. Nobody knew; but it seemed the wisest course not to chance the little voyage. At half-past eleven, to one sitting patiently on a spar under the lee of a shed, there became apparent at the dock entrance a huge dark hull, all studded over with lights, slowly forging forward, amid the shouting of windlass-men and the hoarse words of command, "Slack away, there!" "Tauten that starboard warp!" and such like. It was the *Pera*, and she was coming right into dock. So gingerly had the ponderous monster to be dealt

175

with, that it was past midnight before she was along-side the jetty, and the gangway run aboard.

"The *Megæra* men on board?" "Aye, aye, sir," came in response from out the gloom of the foredeck, through which was just visible a close semicircle of faces. In ten minutes more two of the *Megæra* men were comfortably seated by the fireside, splicing the mainbrace in moderation, as they smoked a quiet pipe before beginning their little story. Cautious worthies of northern extraction, they seemed, if one might so phrase it, to have "Baxter on the brain," impressed, as they were, with a belief that was not quite easy to remove, that their entertainer was an emissary direct from the member for Montrose to pump them to their hurt. Disabused of this apprehension, the conversation became much less constrained.

"Bad luck to St Paul's, and to them that sent us there on four ounces a-day," was a toast that might not in a general way be objectionable, but had no great tendency to throw a light on the series of mis-fortunes which ultimately beached the *Megæra* on the island of St Paul's. It was explained, however, as being merely "blowing off steam," and then my friends settled to their work. "There were no com-plaints to the ship's condition after leaving Queens-town?" "No; but among the crew there was con-stant grumbling and apprehension. You see, it wasn't thought seamanlike to complain. Captain Thrupp, after having had up the petty officers, and heard what they had got to say, made his report at Queenstown, and the ship had been inspected and passed there as fit for the voyage. After that, the captain's mouth was shut, and the men warn't going to funk on it, and be

jeered at, even if they were as sure of going to the
bottom as they were sure of a day's grog. It was a
straight upper lip all round ; but some of the chaps—
the married men 'specially—didn't make a very bright
job of it. No ; about the inspection at Queenstown
I won't say nothing good or bad, whether I think it
was a thorough one or a sham. It ain't my place for
to be the judge of my superiors. There was no stoke-
plate taken up for the inspecting officer. Ah, that's
another thing ; if you ask me whether there ought to
have been, I answer that it ain't my place for to say.
Between Queenstown and the Cape we had a good
fair voyage, the ship averaging eight to nine knots.
The weather mostly was splendid ; I think, on my
soul, that God Almighty in His mercy picked the
weather for us on purpose.

"The ship was low in the water, and always
cumbered with overcrowding and stores ; it never
seemed as if it were possible to get everything snug
and shipshape, try how you would. After we left the
Cape, on the 28th of May, the weather, although it
looked threatening sometimes, still stood to us like a
brick ; and on the 7th and 8th of June we lay our
course famously, running under double-reefed taw'sles
and courses before a regular snorer, a strong sea on,
and the whole water now and then coming tumbling
aboard of her. It was that same day that we over-
hauled the Frenchman ; and in the afternoon a marine
was washed overboard. The very next day, the 9th,
we sprung a leak—a devil of a big leak, too,—for the
water came in so that it took the pumps all their time
to keep it under. Some of the chaps swore that the
sodger, as he went to the bottom, had sent his knee

M

through one of the plates; others would have it that
he stuck his bayonet in her; but that couldn't have
been, because the man didn't take his bayonet overboard with him.   All hands at the pumps; and by
good luck, there being plenty of pumps, we managed
to keep the leak a bit under.   But it wasn't to be found
nohow.   It was a time, I can tell you.   A gale of wind,
the old b—— deep in the water, and rolling taw'sle-
yard stun'sle-booms under at every second roll; all
hands, blue jackets and marines, working their hearts
out at the pumps—always wet, and not a chance to
get dry.   Day and night it was alike, till after three
days of it the men were fairly beat out, and we had
to take to the fire-engine and the donkey-engine to
keep the water down.

"It was Jock Brown, 'Scottie' we call him, that
found the leak.   Scottie was one of the leading stokers.
It was on the night of the 13th June.   He had the
first watch in the engine-room, and had to report the
state of the pumps every half-hour to the officer of
the watch.   Scottie took it into his head to find the
leak if he could.   The bunkers had been in the way
of a search round about below them; it would have
been necessary to shift the coals from port to starboard and then back again, and hands could not well
be spared.   But Scottie got about the bilges by the
beam on which the bunkers rest that crosses the ship
above the mid-girder.   Scottie shoved his head down
one hole and his light down another, and there, in
one of the plates under the bunkers—not under the
engines—was the water coming streaming in like a
waterspout.   He called the officer of the watch, and
told him he had found the leak.   'Where?' shouts

the officer. 'Come, and I'll show you.' Mr ——
came, had a long look for himself, head down one
hole, light down another, and then goes and rouses
up the 'Old Man.' The 'Old Man' comes double-
quick, lies down—we had spread a mat for him—and
bides a long time with his head out of sight. At last
he comes to the surface, and turning to the stoker on
duty, says, 'Have you called Mr Mills?' 'No, sir,'
says the stoker, 'he has not turned in for three nights
before, and I was giving him a chance.' 'Call him at
once,' says the Old Man. I was sent for Mr Mills.
Mr Mills is the chief engineer. Up the passage by
the sentry handy the wheel I went, and called him.
'Leak found, sir!'

It was not many minutes before Mr Mills and
the Old Man had their heads together. They con-
sulted for a spell, and then the word was, 'Fetch
Jamie Hares, the artificer.' Then the ratchet-brace
was sent for, and a piece was to be drilled out of
a girder that was in the way, so as to let a man's
hand in to reach the hole in the plate. I'll finish off
the yarn of the leak before I talk about anything else.
An inside sheeting of gutta percha clapped fast with
a hot shovel was first tried; but that was stove in as
soon as the ship got way on her, and the water began
to press harder on her outside. Then Bell, the diver
—he belongs to the *Excellent*—went over the side,
and brought up word that the skin of the ship was
like a rotten honeycomb. It was not so nonsensical
after all, for the chaps to hold that the sinking marine
sent his knee through the plate, for Bell said he could
send the heel of his boot through it with quite a
moderate kick. He went down with a plate for the

outside, while a corresponding plate was clapped on inwardly, holes drilled in the original plate, and a trial made to screw the outer and inner plates down to it. But, Lord bless you, the infernal thing was so thin and worn that the nuts could not be screwed home, and so the jury-plates could not be fastened down. And besides, the bottom was so rotten that the new plates—stuck on to it by the screws, and working loosely as they did for want of purchase for the rivets—threatened every minute as if they would tear the old plate right out. There's a bit in the Bible somewhere about putting new wine into old bottles. Here was the same thing for all the world, and the new iron was too strong for the old, rotten, spongy iron, honeycombed with rust. My own amazement is how the old tub could have kept going so long without her engines tumbling through the ship's bottom." " By G——, chum," put in here the " silent member," who had as yet only come out strong in consuming his grog and nodding vigorous confirmation to the statements of his comrade, " By G——, chum, it licks me how the bottom itself did not tumble clean away from the ship !"

" The leak and the rotten plates were bad enough ; but perhaps worse was to come. The girders or ribs —I see you know little about a ship, sir—are the frame or skeleton of the ship, the iron plates bolted on to them, and to one another, being the skin. A ship is just like an open umbrella, the whalebones are the girders or ribs ; the silk "—— " Gingham it may be, sir," puts in the " silent member" rather disparagingly, as it seemed, as to my familiarity with a silk umbrella. " The silk is the skin. These girders are about eighteen inches apart. On four of them rests the step of the mast—in other words, on these four girders, two forward and two aft of the step, there comes nearly the whole weight of the heavy mast, with all that belongs to it. This weight is so distributed as to spare any one single girder; for it is, I tell you, a severe and sudden trial when a ship is suddenly taken aback, and then the downward push of the mast on to its bed is very great. Well, sir, one of the leading stokers—on the 18th of June, I think, this was—found that these four girders, instead of supporting the step of the mast, as they should have done, had decayed and rotted away for a good distance all around the step, so that the mast actually rested and leant all its weight, not on the ribs of the ship, but on its thin and weak skin. You see that there pillar, sir. Well, I reckon, if you were to cut away the flooring you'd find it resting on a good sturdy crossbeam, or, mayhap, its weight distributed over three or four. But suppose there were no cross-beams, or that they were all rotten, and that the pillar rested its own weight and all the weight it supports on the thin planking of the floor, I reckon you'd neither care about being up-stairs or down-stairs. Well, there ain't any down-stairs at sea, only the bottom; and how we are here to-night, instead of there, has amazed me more than tongue can tell ever since I saw the step of that mast." "It licks me hollow, sir, as I may say," put in the silent member. "With all that weight on these rotten plates," continued the other, "what possessed the mast that it did not go right slap through, I can't ever tell; if the ship had been taken aback, it must have gone through just as

a circus rider jumps through a paper hoop.   But as
it was, the weight, although it had not made a hole,
had borne so on the plates, that the bottom had
bulged down, and gone clean away from the rotten
remnants of the girders.   The man that discovered
this state of things was a very quiet, cautious fellow,
who didn't like putting himself forward, so he got
hold of a chap named C——, a noisy, blabbing kind
of chap, who he was sure would have it all over the
ship in no time.   'What d'ye want?' says C——.
'Come and look at this,' says the other.   C——
went, and after a bit of a look we heard his roar, 'By
G——, the bottom's gone from the girders!'   C——
makes a rush for the chief engineer.   'Where's this
d——d place?' asked he, when, puffing and blowing
—he is stout, is the chief engineer—he got down.
He was shown it, and the quiet man told him about
having found it, and got a jacketing for not having
come direct and reported it at once.   'Do you wish
us all to go to the bottom at any minute?' was the
question of the chief engineer.   The captain was
fetched, and made a close examination.   I once
knew a chap so bad in consumption that he said
he was spitting himself bodily away as he walked.
Blessed if the *Megæra* warn't, after a fashion, spitting
herself away as she steamed.   The suction of the
pumps was like the poor fellow's cough; it fetched
pieces of the rotten girders up the pumps, and so out
into the sea.   But the fragments of her pretty well
choked the pumps at last, for the Old Man found
them obstructed with a lot of the old iron that had
not gone up the spout.   Ten minutes after his inspection was over, the ship was condemned.

"You'll search the navy over, sir, before you'll find a better seaman or a truer officer than our Old Man." "By ——, sir, he's in the right on't there," interpolated the silent member. "You should have heard him reading prayers that Sunday forenoon. There warn't a shake in his voice, no more than if he were going below presently for a glass of grog, instead of having it on his mind to tell his ship's company that his ship might go down at any moment. He ain't much a speaker, ain't the Old Man; but his words got pretty nigh men's hearts that day. He told us how that 'the ship's bottom was literally dropping out,' and then bade us go in with a will like men and British sailors. We gave him three cheers, and then we went at it, and started out a considerable lot of grub that Sunday afternoon and evening.

"But with the night came dirty weather. She began dragging her anchors, and at length they parted two of them, and we had to get up a full head of steam to keep the ship off the rocks. The wind was so strong that the old ship—she was always a crabbed, awkward —— at minding her helm—once yawed right round, and was going stem on upon the breakers. The captain got her out of this trouble by going full speed astern, but there she was, right out of hand, only one anchor left, and deep water under her, where not a soul could have been saved had she foundered. Boats? the boats could not have lived over the bar. And what a lot of boats she had! Why, sir, some of them were as old as herself, and there was not accommodation in them for above two-thirds of those on board.

"So the skipper gave the word to run her on shore,

and chance it. It was the afternoon of the 19th of June, about half-past one, that the word was given, 'All hands on deck,' and the ship's head slewed round to the landward. The hands were ordered on deck so as to give them a chance should she strike the bar as everybody feared. Half the crew were on the topgallant fok'sle, half aft, every man ready for a spring if she should break her back. Between the rollers and the sharks, I fear it would have gone hard ' with them. Where was I? Oh, below, for some-body had to keep the steam on. The stokers were forced to remain below. At least it warn't altogether force, but duty, sir; for we never thought to grumble, although we never thought to see the deck again. Orders were to get on a very strong head of steam. The glands were leaking, and I thought every minute the steam-pipe would go." "Hadn't we got souls to be saved like the rest?" struck in the silent member. "They never so much as asked us to drink, but stuck us in the dangerousest place in the whole ship, and left us there to take our chance. My hair, I know, was a-standing straight on end." "Why, don't own that you funked it, old chap," said the other; and then, turning to the writer, continued, "But it was an anxious moment. We talked down there about things sailors don't often talk about. The engineer contended that as we were down below on duty, and for the common good, we should be pretty sure of heaven if the burst-up should come. Then as we neared the bar we shook hands and parted, each man turning his face to the wall.

"She cleared the bar, and took the ground beauti-ful. She went on the rocks as smooth and easy as if she had been an empty egg-shell. If she had been a sound, strong ship, her masts would have gone by the board with the shock ; but she was so rotten that there was no shock, and the rocks came up through her as if her bottom had been of pie-crust.

" Most of the marines went ashore on the 19th, but the general landing-day was the 20th. That night everybody slept on the sod, wet as all were—for the most of the work was up to the waist in water. No mistake, officers and men went in manfully together. There was no favouring the rank, that there time, for the rank scorned to be favoured. All fared alike, and fared thundering rough, too, I can tell you. We began to be rationed on the short allowance on the 20th—6 oz. biscuit, ½ lb. salt meat, half allowance of sugar and cocoa, and half a gill of ' squaro.' Afterwards the bread ration was reduced to four ounces. In a day or two tents of one kind or another began to be rigged up, and some night's shelter was to be had. Working day and night, it was trying to have but a pint of water a day for the whole of the first week. Of the goats killed, the officers had a share as well as the men. The messman had a good quantity of stores of various kinds, which the men, during the voyage, might have of by purchase, but on the island he was not allowed to dispose of any more. By the way, these stores are left on the island, and we might as well have had a share of them. But then, it is true, the Old Man was not to know that we should be there for so short a time ; and I don't doubt, as you say, sir, that he did everything for the best. I haven't an ill word to say against any officer of the ship.

"After we had been there about a month, the first ship came—the Dutchman in which Lieutenant Jones went to Batavia. The next ship was also a Dutchman, which took off some of the officers and boys. Some of the boys lost their kits, and there was a subscription for them among the men to buy them new ones. I think we ought to be repaid that there by Government, sir. Then came an English ship, which gave us some flour, and afterwards the *Taunton*, followed by the *Malacca* and the *Rinaldo*. Then came a severe gale, in which both the *Malacca* and *Rinaldo* were blown off, but the *Rinaldo* was blown furthest. The embarkation in the former was going forward when the latter reappeared, and signalised that all hands should embark on the *Malacca*, which we did, and sailed from St Paul's amid three rousing cheers from the *Rinaldo*. The Old Man was the last to leave the island, as he had been the last to leave the *Megæra*. And now, sir, I must leave you, for our orders are to muster at nine, and I want a couple or three hours' sleep before then. The *Malacca* took us to King George's Sound ; then we came by the *Geelong* to Point de Galle, and so home. The P. and O. people treated us like princes ; nothing was too good for us, beef and beer to the mast-head."

A MARCH ON BRIGHTON.

A MARCH ON BRIGHTON.

(TO AN EASTER-MONDAY REVIEW.)

THURSDAY was the eve of our march, and far and wide had gone the postman bearing the fiery cross, with the order for our mobilisation inscribed on a halfpenny post-card. Our mobilisation, as regards its details, consisted mainly in looking to the buttons of gaiters, in greasing highlows, in making our last wills and testaments in case of accidents, in compounding cunning mixtures for the field flask, and in fondly kissing the babies whom, when the morrow's sun should dawn, we should leave slumbering sweetly the sleep of innocence, while their male parents strode forth to "horrid war." It is an important axiom in war that the invader should utilise to the utmost any rapid means of locomotion which he may find in the hostile territory. He would be justified in thus diverting from its humble but useful calling a metropolitan tramway. We have seen in the late war of how much value to the Germans were the French railroads. Our Commander-in-Chief was fully alive to the advantages accruing from availing himself of a line of railway which, having its home terminus at London Bridge, penetrated the enemy's country some distance.

189

Irrepressible Uhlans, in the guise of station-masters and staff officers who, to serve their country, had donned the humble moleskin of the railway porter, had pioneered this line as far as a place called Redhill, and calling into exercise the telegraph, that potent engine in war, had communicated to our chief the important information that he might safely use this railway during the section of his advance, intervening between London Bridge and Redhill. The hour fixed for the general rendezvous was nine o'clock in the morning of Friday the 7th of April. As the serried columns converged on the rendezvous, their martial tread and gallant bearing must have rejoiced the souls of the numerous burghers looking out of window ; but the chief overt display of national feeling was on the part of three patriotic small boys in Wellington Street, in one of whom patriotic ardour took the peculiar form of turning the youth in question upside down. In point of fact, he surveyed us standing on his head. The second confined himself to uttering the exclamation " Hooray !" at brief intervals ; while the third pressed on the soldiers of his country love gifts in the shape of fusee-boxes, his disinterestedness being, however, somewhat sullied by the fact that he craved base copper in return for the boxes. But, as we know, human nature is weak, especially in boys. The great majority having provided themselves with copies of the London news-papers as a means for civilising the benighted people in the enemy's country, the troops were expeditiously and safely embarked, and the train rolled out of the London Bridge Station at five minutes past nine.

It occurs to me that up till now I have given no

details regarding the composition of the army of whose deeds I am about to record the history. This omission demands immediate remedy. Our Commander-in-Chief was Major Smith Richards, the chief of his staff being Captain Wyatt. His divisional commanders were Captains Lyon, Moberly, and Stedall, who had respectively under them five officers of inferior rank—gentlemen of ardour, energy, and perseverance. The army of which these were the officers consisted of the drums and fifes and three companies of the 37th Middlesex Rifle Volunteers, one of the strongest and most efficient of the metropolitan volunteer corps.

On emerging from the station at Redhill, we were formed up on the esplanade, and the preliminary arrangements were expeditiously made. Our field train, consisting of a baggage and a proviant waggon in one, was judiciously parked meanwhile in a side street under a baggage-guard of sufficient strength. As we marched off the esplanade and through the little town, dense masses of the population crowded upon our flanks with so much persistency, that it required great self-control on the part of our soldiers to restrain themselves from reprisals. No doubt there was a deep design in these tactics of the Redhill natives. Hate against the invader was presumably rankling in their hearts, but with a dissimulation which made one sigh over the falsity of human nature, they effectually dissembled their hostile feelings, and when they jostled us it was with a smile and a laugh —as often as not a horse laugh. Their females took part in the plot, bringing out their babies and older children, that the sight might lull us into a treacherous security, while the men gradually mingling in our ranks should change their tactics on a preconceived signal, and strive to take us unawares.   However, the steadiness, discipline, and self-restraint of our men baulked those fell intentions, and without any mishap we gained the open expanse of Earlswood Common, on which we immediately deployed, throwing out clouds of skirmishers to clear the front.

Some of our men who had made a special study of the social geography of the enemy's country, pointed out a large building in the vicinity of this common as an establishment, the interior of which was the most fitting place for some of their comrades.   The allusion was very recondite, and did not appear to be generally understood.   Perhaps it was not complimentary, and therefore great effort was not made to comprehend it.   At the end of the first three miles the army halted, as per regulation, for a breathing space of five minutes, and advantage was taken of this relaxation to uncork numerous "water-bottles," not one of which, so far as I could learn, contained water.   Their con-tents were remarkably diversified, from tea that had once been pleasant and cold, but was now lukewarm and impregnated with the bi-phospho-sulphate of block tin, which the action of the tea had chemically extracted from the metal of the flask.   The beverage which seemed to gain the warmest encomiums was a glutinous fluid bearing a marked resemblance to salad-dressing, which its possessor recommended as being "at once meat and drink"—a statement fully borne out by personal experience.   Huge profits are, in my opinion, to be made by patenting this mixture under some high-sounding name of some eighteen syllables ; but its disinterested inventor wholly repudiated the suggestion, as, in the first place he is, like Mr Macfie, opposed on principle to the Patent Acts ; and, secondly, because he could not think of withholding from his fellow-men the beatific results of his researches into the mysteries of compounding "good drinks." Acting in this spirit, he commissioned me to give publicity to the recipe, which is as follows :—Half a pint of good milk, two glasses and a half of dry sherry, one glass of brandy, and two eggs beaten up in the fluid. The time may come when a grateful country will vote a statue to the benefactor who enabled me to place this recipe at its disposal ; but the suggestion at present might be regarded as a little premature.

Just as the bugle sounded "Stand to your arms," something of a suspicious character was noticed in the rear of a hillock on our left front. The advance guard were equal to the occasion ; dispersing into very open order they proceeded cautiously forward much in the manner of deer-stalkers, the officer who occupied the most advanced position in the centre making herculean efforts to look round a corner. Not being able to achieve this successfully, he wisely halted his force till the reserve came up, his dispositions in the meantime being made with great discretion to resist any sudden "ugly rush" on the part of an enemy. No rush, however, ugly or otherwise, was attempted. The suspicious object, which certainly bore a remarkable resemblance to a vidette circling on an enemy's front, turned out to be an animal of the bovine species tied to a stump, around which she was sedulously gyrating. Being a national army,

N

not a licentious professional soldiery, we carefully refrained from offering any injury or indignity to the wretched inhabitants of a territory already smitten sufficiently through the paralysis of a hostile invasion.

The stagnation of all trade was apparent in the closed shutters of the shops, which one of the staff, with a frivolity unworthy of his position, strove to assign to the circumstance that a sacred day known as " Good Friday" was kept in those parts with much strictness. We were no Dugald Dalgettys, no swashbuckler mercenaries, the sheen of our valour tarnished by greed and debauchery. In the bad old wars the path of an invasion was marked by fire and sword ; by the corpses of inoffensive villagers slaughtered for their filthy lucre ; by outraged womanhood and scared children ; while the hamlets protested to heaven with smoke and flame against the barbarities of fiends in human shape. On our advance, maid and matron gazed without fear, nay, even with a modest boldness, which was surely a grand compliment to our civilisation. Candour compels me to add that one of the drums and fifes was detected *flagrante delicto* in winking at a daughter of the Amalekite, and the treacherous syren was observed, Delilah-like, to smile upon the youth in return. This was a symptom of incipient demoralisation that demanded an exemplary example to prevent its spread, and the misguided youth was justly sentenced to whistle without interruption for half an hour—an appropriate punishment, seeing that it is impossible for the most pliable-featured individual to smile and to whistle simultaneously.

On our approach to the little river Mole, our *éclaireurs* were sent forward to reconnoitre its banks, and no doubt had we been provided with a pontoon train it would have followed. The banks were reported, however, as clear from obstruction, and a bridge was discovered which the enemy in his flight had neglected to blow up, and on which we crossed with safety and despatch.

Lowfield Heath is hitherto unknown to fame, so far as I am aware. It contains a population of about fifty-two souls, of which a large proportion consists of children, and there is, too, a sprinkling of gaffers very red as to nose, very wide as to mouth, and strongly developed in the region of highlows. Lowfield Heath contains also a gentleman who may be described as a cosmopolitan philanthropist. We were foes, it was true, but were also fellow human beings, and he felt for us as men, while no doubt his patriotism led him to hate us as enemies. We were dusty, we were hungry, we were thirsty. But for him our forenoon halt would have taken place in the road. But he knew of a snug little triangular field, secluded behind lofty hedges, and thither he magnanimously guided first our field train, and then the columns of fighting-men.

The tailboard of the proviant waggon was let down, and an energetic quartermaster - sergeant proceeded to discharge its contents. A colossal cheese came out first. It was followed by a large assortment of zinc pails, which suggested to the natives who were spectators that the army was about to wash its feet, and counter suggestions were freely offered as to the alleged superior advantages of a running brook in the neighbourhood. I heard a matron, the milk of human kindness swelling high in her portly bosom, as she talked with her gossip, wonder whether the "pore fellows" had got towels. Then came several pots of great size and extreme sootiness, and after them a tea-chest.   The latter apparition appeared to engender among the natives a bare suspicion that we martialists had it in view to set up a chandler's shop in opposition to the local dealer, who, in addition to a trade in "sundries," appeared to do business in tiles and fire extinguishing ; and who, the general opinion was, as expressed with a certain morose satisfaction, would be compelled to put his shutters up at once, and betake himself to bed, stricken with an attack of jaundice, arising from jealousy.

After the tea-chest came the headquarter flag, which, under a guard of honour, was carefully stuck in the hedge, from which it floated out proudly on the breeze, to the discomfiture, doubtless, of the lurking Francs - Tireurs who, from the distant heights, were presumably watching with black dismay in their caitiff hearts the rapid and irresistible progress of the invading host.   No precautions were omitted to prevent these gentry from interfering with the mid-day meal of bread, cheese, and beer, the latter requisitioned from a wayside inn, where, in times of peace, as we were given to understand, an institution widely known in the enemy's country as the "Brighton Coach" is wont to stop on its daily journey for lunch.   It is, by the way, an illustration of the loathsomely mercenary character of the inhabitants of the unhappy country which now lies prostrate at our feet, that, as we were given to understand, while the halt of this vehicle for eating pur-

poses is only twenty minutes, sundry of the viands
are served in a state of diabolical heat, demanding
quite a quarter of an hour's dispersion of caloric
before they attain an edible condition. Our outposts
were located in eligible positions in the vicinity of
the bivouac, and you may be sure that a strong
position afforded by an adjacent windmill was not
neglected.

When the arrangements had been completed by the
quartermaster's department, the cosmopolitan philanthropist already referred to courteously approached
the Commander-in-Chief, and invited him and all the
officers of the army to lunch in his adjacent villa.
This gentleman, perhaps, had the fear of rigorous
requisitions before his eyes. If so, his apprehensions
were groundless. He, and the ladies of his family,
instead of flying in vague terror when the sun glinted
on the bayonets of our advanced guard as it topped
the hill commanding the heath, had courageously remained at home, and under those circumstances their
residence and its belongings would have been scrupulously respected. As it was, his hearty invitation
was accepted in the spirit in which it was given. We
war with nations and armies, not with individuals.
Proceeding in a body to this hospitable mansion, the
officers found an excellent cold luncheon displayed on
an ample board, and full justice was done to the good
things provided, the pleasure of the entertainment being
enhanced by the circumstance that the ladies of the
house, instead of sequestrating themselves in their
harem, honoured us with their presence. As a consequence of our admirable system of national education,
we were all quite familiar with the language of the

country, and an hour, which I sincerely trust was pleasant to both sides, as it certainly was to one, slipped rapidly away. When the sixty minutes had fleeted by, the Commander-in-Chief, who is a relentless disciplinarian, caused "officers' call" to be peremptorily sounded, and in a few minutes more the army was again on its march.

Nothing of importance occurred till we approached a village designated on our staff maps as Crawley, and here the aspect of affairs was decidedly threatening. Appearances seemed to indicate that a barricade had been erected just outside the village, and the heads and shoulders of truculent-looking villagers seemed to loom formidably over the obstruction. As we drew nearer it became apparent that what we had taken for a barricade was but an accumulation of small boys; and when the population came to recognise our strength, they assumed what were no doubt hypocritical grins of welcome, the females in particular wearing syren smiles, intended, probably, to lure us to our destruction. But we stoically resisted the insidious attraction, and marched steadily forward. As we strode up the village, it became apparent that the windows were densely lined with the inhabitants who, questionless, had meditated making a street fight of it, and pouring down volleys from their elevated positions on our devoted heads. But at this crisis our drums and fifes struck up with opportune boisterousness, and their martial din, combined with our resolute bearing, struck terror into the people, and enabled us to pass through the village, and, indeed, through the toll-bar at its further end, without let or hindrance. Then we got into the defiles of Crawley Forest, where great

caution was requisite ; but our flanking patrols were
equal to the emergency, although I grieve to state
that at this stage of our march, it became apparent
that the baggage-guard had become demoralised, and
had mounted the waggon in the most reprehensible
manner. A halt on the top of the hill admitted of the
light division, consisting of three men and an officer,
clearing the front in a highly satisfactory manner; and
it was thus with the utmost confidence that we again
stood to our arms, and marched on through the most
intricate recesses of the forest. This episode showed
the advantage of having a thoroughly efficient light
division to cover the front and flanks.

As we breasted the last slope the word was passed
along the column, "Singers to the front ;" and a
variety of ditties, chiefly with strongly accentuated
choruses, were indulged in, the ingenuous youth com-
posing the drums and fifes mainly giving the tone to
the harmony. It was good to hear the "Men of
Merry England" and "Rule Britannia" echoing
through the glades of a hostile forest, and a subaltern
of an imaginary turn of mind amused himself by con-
juring up spectacles of the invisible enemy, gnashing
their teeth and hissing hot curses as the cheery sounds
reached them from the throats of the advancing co-
horts from Bloomsbury. One man there was in the
army whose soul these strains did not delight—an
individual of a misanthropical idiosyncracy ; a saturnine party, into whose soul the iron of a rejection by
a fair one was reported to have entered, and who
looked upon jollity with a jaundiced eye, nor took
delight in companionship. Even he—the sad, saturnine, solitary cynic—even he found his part in the

abounding resources of our administration.   He had
the post, and he seemed to enjoy it, of acting singly as
the connecting-link between the advanced guard and
the main body.   There, as he strode on alone, he might
commune uninterruptedly with his grief, and smile
sardonically as, at a turn when the wind blew his way,
the discordant sounds of mirth were wafted to his ears.

At Handcross, where there is an open common, a
cricket club presented a sinister aspect, and prompt
intimidatory measures were called for.   You never
know what are the insidious designs of the subtle-
minded foe, and it is always well to err on the safe
side ; so the order was given for the advanced guard
and a strong party from the main column to extend
in skirmishing order.   Now was the time for the solitary connecting-link to distinguish himself, and the
assiduous manner in which he extended single-handed
in open order deserved to earn him the respect of his
fellow-countrymen.   The cricket club wisely developed an unbellicose disposition, and without molesting
them, we drew in our skirmishers and pressed steadily
on.   Soon after, the length of the march began to tell
on Private Fitzhighlows, who was presently compelled
to fall out and betake himself to the proviant-train, in
consequence of having incautiously taken the field in
new boots.   As his comrades defiled past him, he was
heard to express a valorous resolve to telegraph to his
mother to send him out an old and roomy pair of
boots by the feld-post   It is to be hoped that she
will send both boots in one parcel, since, in case of
the miscarriage of one boot, the consequences would
be similar to those attending the half of a pair of
drawers received per the same medium by "Kutseke."

We passed Cuckfield without molestation or incident,

and presently reached Hayward's Heath, where, having marched twenty-one miles, it was deemed advisable to quarter the army for the night. As we came down the slope, some lovers of nature observed with rapture the effect of the setting sun as he sank to rest over the top of the workhouse. The host, flushed with victory, was quite prepared to bivouac "under the beautiful stars," but a large market-house opportunely was found, which, when bedded down with straw, formed eligible quarters. The staff and other officers were excellently accommodated in the adjacent Station Hotel. The most careful precautions were taken against a night surprise. A sufficiency of out-lying sentries were posted, and to insure vigilance the reliefs took place every hour, under the superintendence of a divisional commanding-officer, while each division had its hour of duty ; and the Commander-in-Chief, with praiseworthy solicitude for the safety of his men, made the grand rounds more than once during the night. The men did their own cooking, and the military commissariat was amply sufficient for the demands made upon it. The band boys, however, whose first campaign this was, persisted in singing noisy ditties through the livelong night, thereby subjecting themselves to becoming cockshies for the veteran soldiers, who vented their disgust through the medium of boots and other articles as missiles, unfortunately not productive of the desired effect.

In the evening the army was overtaken by its highly efficient medical organisation, in the person of Dr Meyer; but his services were fortunately not called into requisition. At nine next morning the march was resumed. Private Fitzhighlows, having judiciously had his boots lasted and rubbed with dubbing overnight, was himself again in the morning, and marched as well as the best.   Nothing occurred worthy of note, the foe having evidently become utterly demoralised by the rapidity of our advance. At Pykehain took place the forenoon halt, where the benevolent wife of a farmer supplied the army with milk *à discretion*—beer for those who preferred it being requisitioned from a neighbouring public-house. Toward four o'clock in the afternoon, the outskirts of the hostile capital were triumphantly reached.   On the part of what had been presumably its garrison, curiosity prevailed over shame.   Dressed in uniform, but denuded of their arms, the men of various regiments thronged the side-walks, gazing with undisguised curiosity on our dusty but undaunted array. It was a striking instance of the milk-and-water-spirited abjectness of the civilian population that from several houses fluttered flags bearing the word "Welcome."   Among the disorganised bands of unarmed men we observed some bearded stragglers wearing a strange and peculiar costume, consisting of short grey petticoats, which showed a portion of bare knee below.   Others were arrayed in red, and yet others in green, but all had apparently relinquished any hostile intentions, and indeed professed what was no doubt a spurious admiration of our serviceable appearance.   And so, to our military music, we reached a terrace by the sea, and observing a good-looking hotel bearing the name of the "Queen's," we proceeded to requisition there accommodation for headquarters, while the army was billeted throughout the town.   Our triumph was consummated ; and, not being braggarts, we leave it to a discerning world and to posterity to recognise our merits.

F U R S.

FURS.

THE Earl of Dorset began a sea-song, written on the
eve of battle, with an apostrophe "To all ye ladies
now on land." On this occasion we make our bow
to all the ladies, whether on the land or on the sea—
mainly the sea of fashion ; and we would respectfully
address them thus :—" O fair creatures, young and
old, when the stormy winds do blow, and when the
dictates of Dame Fashion prompt, and you betake
yourselves to Poland's or Nicolay's, or Drake's, or
Wayre's, and there invest, regardless of expense, in
fur jackets, tippets, muffs, cuffs, edgings, trimmings,
and all the furry etceteras of feminine fashionable
costume, mysteries recondite unto the masculine
understanding, do you ever care to exercise the brains
inside the pretty heads as to whence come all the
furs which contribute to your luxury—how they come
into the hands of those who sell them to you, and
what they are like before they are tittivated into the
condition in which you buy them ?" Taking it for
granted that you do develop some curiosity in this
direction, and care to know something on the subject
of the trade in furs generally, the uses to which the
numerous varieties are devoted, and the prices which
they fetch in their raw state, be it known that this

article is devoted to the purpose of enlightening you
thereanent.

Let us first visit a huge pile of warehouses in Lime
Street, the very heart of the City. Great waggons
are unloading square canvas-trussed bales and pack-
ages, which are being hoisted up to the various floors
of the warehouses. The Hudson Bay Company are
garnering their harvest. Each of these bales has
been a great traveller. The skins of which it is com-
posed are from one of the many forts and stations
which stud that vast tract of Northern America still
known as the Hudson Bay Territory. One batch is
from York Fort, another from the Mackenzie River,
a third from Labrador, a fourth from the interior of
Greenland, a fifth from Arthabasca, a sixth from the
eastern fringe of the Rocky Mountains, a seventh from
the Saskatchewan, an eighth from British Columbia,
a ninth from Vancouver's Island ; and these are only
a few of the principal stations. They have come to
England in the Company's own vessels, and are now
being placed in the Company's warehouses and show-
rooms. Inside, amid that peculiar half-pungent dried-
meat odour which raw furs give out, sagacious, ab-
sorbed men are sorting the skins as they are unpacked.
A glance, a brush with the hand against the grain of
the fur, are all that is needed to distinguish the
quality ere the skin is thrown on the pile of " firsts,"
" seconds," or " thirds " to which it is entitled to be-
long. Other men make them up in lots, and place
them in their proper places ; the catalogue is printed,
and the sale advertised. Of these there are two, the
spring and the autumn; the first in March, the second
in September. Then the show-rooms are crowded
with a motley horde of buyers of various nationalities,

but all distinguished by the double emblem of a catalogue in the hand and a white over-blouse on the body to protect the clothes from the grease and hair of the skins.

The first room into which our conductor ushers us is the " bear-room." Literal " bear-garden " as it is, —for 5000 bears are represented in it by their skins, —it is quieter than could be the St Pancras Board of Guardians, had every one of its members pledged themselves to brotherly love. But what a scene this bear-room would be, to be sure, if every skin were to be rehabilitated by its living occupant, and 5000 bears —grizzly, polar, brown, black, and grey—were to spring into sudden vitality! Very soon we find that the value of bear-skins is in the inverse ratio to their size and to the ferocity of the animals in life. Here is the skin of a polar bear that measures 10 feet by 7. When alive, the huge rascal most likely frightened many a peaceful whaler ; but now mankind has its revenge upon him. He may think himself lucky if his shaggy white hide sells for a pound, and men will wipe their feet on the skin of him at which they would have shuddered when alive. *Sic transit.* Nor does the formidable " grizzly" fare much better in the fur-market. His fierceness and his rarity combined make his skin a scarce commodity—there are only 300 grizzlies in the room ; but he goes dirt-cheap for all his scarceness, and his pell is chiefly used in the manufacture of artists' brushes, the long hair being pulled out for this purpose. There was a time—it is about twenty-five years ago, so of course none of the ladies can remember it—when the brown bear was in high favour with the fair sex. His fur was very fashionably displayed as a narrow trimming round

the edges of shawls. In these palmy days a fine
" cinnamon" bearskin was worth thirty guineas. But
capricious fashion has altered, and now the best
" brown" strives in vain to fetch £3, 10s. The
" black" bears of good quality will maintain their
price (about £5 for a first-class skin) so long as the
authorities, in the plenitude of their wisdom, thatch
the heads of our guardsmen with wickerwork baskets
covered with bearskin. Officers' bearskins are made
from " yearlings" and " cubs," relatively to their size
the most valuable of all black bear-skins.

In the next room is quite a menagerie of foxes—
crop fox, red fox, bastard fox, Arctic fox, kitt or
prairie fox, blue fox. The crop fox is grey, with a
tinge of red and silver. A good skin is worth 48s. ;
and he is chiefly used for muffs and cloak-linings.
The red fox is a tawny animal, shading away into a
bright yellow on the sides, and with a white belly.
The darker and richer the fur, the greater the value ;
but 14s. will buy the best of the red foxes, which are
also mostly made into muffs, the lower qualities being
dyed and used for cloak-linings. The Arctic fox has
a beautiful fur, pure snowy white, the best of them
preserving that hue right down to the skin, " blowing
white to the ground," as it is technically called. The
pile is very thick, soft, and close, and it is one of the
warmest of furs. The prairie or kitt fox is a shabby
little beast, about the size of a hare, with poor, woolly,
grey fur, which is used for common cloak-linings and
the lower classes of chaise-wrappers. Here in a
corner are some otter-skins, with nice, short, soft fur,
carrying a beautiful gloss. The blacker they are the
better. Pretty as they are, ladies have not much
reason to regard them with favour. They are cheap

in comparison with fur-seal, and are too often used to imitate that article in the manufacture of professedly "real seal-skin" cloaks. Thus, madam, your "real seal-skin jackets" may only be "real otter." They are also used by gentlemen for coat-collars and fur greatcoats, more especially on the Continent. It will not do to confound between the "otter" and the "sea otter." If a lady could get a jacket of "sea otter" in a mistake for fur-seal, she would be a wise woman to hold her tongue (if possible in the nature of things), and not complain of her bargain. The "sea otter" is the costliest of all fur. A skin that you might put in your hat, or carry away in your muff, has sold for £50; and although this was a fancy price, from £30 to £40 is nothing out of the way. The value is reckoned by the depth of the black colour, studded with silvery hairs, and the richness of the fur. Very seldom do any of the higher qualities come into the retail trade in England, so hungry for them are the Russians. The catch of sea-otter skins is almost entirely confined to the coast of Alaska. When that territory belonged to Russia, the number sent over never exceeded 3000 per annum. Most of the skins went into Russia direct, and the trade was protected by a monopoly. With the transfer of the territory to the United States the monopoly has ceased, and the catch has been doubled within a single year. The same go-ahead policy has been acted upon with regard to fur-seal skins, in which we at home are more directly interested. The old Russian Company used to jog along contentedly, sending to Europe annually about 40,000 fur-seals. During the eighteen months which have elapsed since the transfer, the American successors of the Russian Company have sent to Sir Curtis Lampson, the great consignee of the United States furs, about 300,000 fur-seal skins, representing a money value of about £400,000. A few years of this would go far to re-imburse the purchase-money which our cousins paid to Russia for the sterile tract ; but the best judges are disposed to fear that, in their haste to " realise," our go-ahead friends are imitating the impulsive individual who killed the goose for the sake of the golden egg.

But to return to our gossiping and rather desultory tour through the show-rooms. " The next article," as auctioneers say, that calls for attention is the black or silver fox, the aristocrat of vulpine furs. These beautiful skins are comparatively rare, the Hudson Bay stock being but 816 ; but they rank next in costliness to the sea otter. They have a fine, rich black fur, longish on neck and shoulders, like a lady's ruff, streaked with silver hairs down the back, and becoming quite black underneath. These, at least, are the characteristics of the best skins, which readily fetch £25 each. The highest qualities are bought for the extravagant Russians, among whom the costliest cloaks are lined with them ; and in England and France the medium qualities are used for trimmings. We have seen a cloak lined with black fox that had cost 4000 roubles. Only the jetty bellies had been used, and about fifteen skins had contributed their quota to the extravagance.

Mink, of which in another show-room we light upon a little collection of over 22,000, is a fur that until re-cently was much neglected, being used almost solely for imitating marten. But a revolution of fashion has sent it up in the market. The belles who shine at Saratoga and the White Mountain have taken a fancy to this pretty fur for cuffs, collars, and trimmings of various sorts; and their English sisters are beginning to follow their example. So mink has risen from 8s. to 25s. per skin.

Some of the wolves, which are here in a large variety of colours, are in high repute for rugs, both hearth and carriage. The most sought after for this purpose are the Churchill wolves, so called from an old Hudson Bay post. These skins are all but milk-white, with a sprinkling of blue-black hairs down the back; and the richness and warmth of the fur are quite remarkable. Yet in price they are comparatively moderate. You can buy the finest Churchill wolf-skin for £1 ; of course there is the cost of dressing in addition. Wolverine (the American glutton) is a softer fur than the wolf, but possesses much the same attributes, and sells at a little over the same price. Wolverine are the pest of the trappers. True to their character, they gormandise on the bait set for the smaller and more valuable fur-bearing animals, and either pull their limbs out of the traps or walk away with them without inconvenience. The fur of the lynx, which is largely represented in one of the upper show-rooms, is much used for muffs, ladies' cloak-linings, &c., and is also dyed to imitate the most costly furs. Prices range from 12s. to 4s. per skin. It may be interesting to owners of the domestic cat to know that some common cat-skins from the United States fetch as much as 5s. 6d. per skin. They are chiefly used for ladies' victorines, &c., and probably often do service for a nominally higher-class fur. The "fishers" come from the more southerly regions of the American lake district, Huron, Superior, and Michigan, while the Mouse River Lake is the commonest. Samson's strength lay in his hair; theirs lie in their tails, which were used on the helmets of the Prussian army until superseded by the ugly spike.

Now they are split up, and out of them are made very costly muffs. When we mention that the price of each good fisher-skin ranges from £2 to £2, 10s., and that the tails are by no means large, it will be obvious that a fisher muff is suited only to the longest purse. Of badgers, racoons—the old original 'coon— and skunks—the latter smelling worse than all the scents of Cologne combined, yet made into beautiful caps and muffs—we have not space to speak at length ; nor of the opossum and musquash, both of which, like the skunk and racoon, come chiefly from the United States. To find the great mass of furry imports from this region, and also from Alaska and the various "territories" connected with the States, a visit must be paid to another warehouse, that of Sir Curtis Lampson (the friend of Peabody), in Queen Street, Cheapside. His consignments, exclusively from American collectors, are considerably larger than those of the Company. There is the great show of fur-seal skins, out of which the beautiful cloaks and jackets are made. The seal aristocrats go under the curious name of "wigs," and fetch as much as £2 apiece. If you would make the round, there are still other two fur warehouses to visit—that of Messrs Marais, in College Hill, devoted almost wholly to American furs, and Messrs Culverwell, Brooks, & Co.'s, also in College Hill. These gentlemen's show-rooms may be styled the most sensational in the trade, since they receive consignments so miscellaneous from all quarters of the world. They are specially strong in the bird skins, which have become so fashionable of late years, and their last catalogue comprehended grebe, gull, pelican, swan, dressed geese, ibis, and flamingo skins, necks and wings of tropical birds, humming-birds, birds-of-paradise, and lots more of the pretty feathered creatures where-withal ladies choose to adorn the fronts of their hats. No branch of the skin trade has been so much developed by fashion as that in grebe skins. The great bulk of them come from Odessa, Berdianski, and Constantinople; and the consignment, which is almost exclusively to Messrs Culverwell & Co., is entirely in the hands of the Greek merchants. Ten years ago the supply only reached a few hundreds, and there was no great demand. Now the import is many thousands annually; and within the last two years grebe skins have fetched 10s. apiece. They are slightly retrograding again in public favour. Messrs Culverwell also sell the bulk of the import of African monkey skins, so much in use for muffs. These are of very variable value, but range from 2s. to 8s. It is believed they are much imitated by Angora goat skins. The same firm are consignees of a considerable number of lion, tiger, leopard, and puma skins, and have had in their warehouse the skins of boa-constrictors, crocodiles, armadilloes, and even of an elephant. A room hung round with splendid lion, tiger, and leopard skins, many of them with the formidable head and paws left on, and their grim beauty diversified by white grebe plumage and the brilliant hues of the ibis and flamingo, is a sight worth going to St Mary-axe to see.

It must be remembered that each and all of these collections is submitted to public auction at the half-yearly series of sales in March and September. These sales constitute the sources whence are drawn the supplies of our home manufacturers and retailers, as well as of the continental buyers, who crowd to them to make investments in time for disposal at the great Leipsic fairs at Easter and Michaelmas. But before venturing into the sale-room, we must bore the reader with a few statistics. The value of the furs thus sold is from £650,000 to £850,000 per annum, and the following is a list of the American fur-skins sold by public auction during 1869:—Beaver, 170,500; musquash, 2,233,400; rabbit, 56,500; opossum, 154,000; fur seal, 40,000; otter, 18,000; marten, 106,000; fisher, 13,000; fox (silver), 2500; fox (cross), 7500; fox (red), 73,000; fox (white), 14,500; fox (blue), 350; fox (grey), 28,000; lynx, 83,000; mink, 97,000; bear (black, brown, grey, and white), 12,000; wolf, 11,000; badger, 5000; racoon, 387,000; sea otter, 1600; common cat, 6800; wolverine, 1200; skunk, 111,000. In all, the stupendous number of 3,630,000 skins were sold, representing an equal number of lives taken, besides a good many thousands of unconsidered trifles, such as ermine, chinchilla, squirrel, rabbit, &c., and entirely exclusive of European, Asiatic, and African skins. It is surprising that, in the face of such an animal slaughter, the supply should be maintained as it is.

The Hudson Bay Company hold their sales in their own house, but the other brokers sell in the Commercial Sale-rooms, Mincing Lane.

Climbing up the long staircase to the top of the house, you enter a large room lighted from the roof, with a rostrum along one of its sides, and on the other three seats sloping backward and upward, as in a class-room. These seats are occupied by a company very motley as to nationality. There is the stolid but cute German, the saturnine Russian, the mercurial Frenchman, the lively Pole, with the keen eye and the swart face, the Dane, the Prussian, the Italian, the Greek, the Yankee (no offence at the juxtaposition), Jews of all these diverse nationalities,

and a good solid substratum of the English element—
also profusely streaked with Hebraicon.   The hats
worn by the assembly are as infinite in their variety
of shape as are the faces in variety of expression.   In
the pulpit, the central figure is the broker and auctioneer—a handsome, grey-haired gentleman, an alder-
man, no less, of the city of London ; and on either
side of him sit members of his firm, either partners or
clerks.   The furs have already been inspected by the
buyers in the warehouses, and each man knows what
he wants, and has marked in his catalogue the limit to
which he is prepared to bid.   There is not the semblance of a fur in the sale-room.   The auctioneer
puts up a lot—say the best of the sea otters—
"Twenty pounds," "fifteen pounds," "ten pounds."
At last he finds a bidder at ten pounds; and then, as
fast as he can articulate, rises step by step, at 5s.
a time, till he has reached the limit that any one in
the room is prepared to go.   Down comes the hammer; but no buyer's name is called, and we are lost
in wonderment.   Whence came all the biddings, since
the company was silent, save for an occasional jest, or
a guttural polyglot remark ?   You might stand in the
room a day, and never get at the explanation of this
mystery ; but after all, like most other things, it is
very simple when you know it.   The auctioneer and
his coadjutors quarter the room like look-outs at sea,
each taking upon himself to pick up the biddings in
his own district.   The amount of "rise" at each bid
is marked in the catalogue, and each buyer has a
silent method of his own—preconcerted with the auctioneer—of denoting that he "springs."   One winks,
another nods, a third bites the end of his pen, a fourth
holds up a finger stealthily, a fifth scratches his head,

and so on. Thus the "public" in the sale-room are kept in the dark as to the nature of the investments made by each particular buyer—a point .often of importance in keeping down fractious competition. Sometimes this silent system breeds charges of what is known as "running." A *bona fide* bidder complains that the opposition bidding is mythical, and invented by the auctioneer to enhance the price. But he can retaliate by leaving off, and letting the auctioneer knock the lot down to the mythical bidder, which involves loss to himself; and this is so obvious, that we believe the practice is seldom resorted to. As in the House of Commons, a little joke goes a long way in the fur sale-room. The auctioneer jocularly entreats a foreign buyer named Wolff to show his fellow-feeling for his namesakes by starting the bidding for wolves; and when he complies, there is a cry of "Wolf, wolf!" from all directions. Wolff, however, retaliates when the auctioneer requests him to begin a lot at twenty shillings, by blandly offering. in broken English, a "pennie," and evidently thinks he has made a hit. Then the cats, when they are put up, give occasion to more small wit, the auctioneer grandiloquently describing them as "the only fur England produces;" while the buyers respond by highly creditable "mieaus." The sales last for about three weeks, and then the foreigners—having paid for and uplifted their goods—are off to Leipsic with them with all speed; while the English buyers at once begin the process of manufacture that is required before they are ready for sale to the ladies and others whom we commenced by addressing.

CHRISTMAS IN A CAVALRY REGIMENT.

CHRISTMAS IN A CAVALRY REGIMENT.

THE civilian world, even that portion of it which lives by the profusest sweat of its brow, enjoys an occasional holiday in the course of the year besides Christmas-day. Good Friday brings to most an enforced cessation from toil. Easter and Whitsuntide are recognised seasons of pleasure in most grades of the civilian community. There are few who do not compass somehow an occasional Derby-day; and we may safely aver that the amount of work done on New Year's-day is not very great. But in all the year the soldier has but one real holiday, a holiday with all the glorious accompaniments of unwonted varieties of dainties and full liberty to be as jolly as he pleases without fear of the consequences. True, the individual soldier may have his day's leave, nay, his month's furlough; but his enjoyments resulting therefrom are not realised in the atmosphere of the barrack-room, but rather have their origin in the abandonment for the nonce of his military character, and a *pro tempore* return into civilian life. Christmas-day is the great regimental merry-making, free to and appreciated by the veteran and the recruit alike; and as such it is looked forward to for many a month

219

prior to its advent, and talked of many a day after it is past and gone.

About a month before Christmas, the observer skilled in the signs of the times may begin to notice the tokens of its approach. Self-deniant fellows, men who can trust themselves to carry a few shillings about with them without experiencing a chronic sensation that the accumulated pelf is burning a hole in their pockets, busy themselves in constructing " dimmocking bags" for the occasion, such being the barrack-room term for receptacles for money-hoarding purposes. The weak vessels, those who mistrust their own constancy under the varied temptations of dry throats, empty stomachs, and a scant allowance of tobacco, manage to cheat their fragility of " saving grace " by requesting their sergeant-major to put them " on the peg ;"—that is to say, place them under stoppages, so that the accumulation takes place in his hands, and cannot be dissipated by any premature weaknesses of the flesh. Everybody becomes of a sudden astonishingly sober and steady. There is hardly any going out of barracks now ; for a walk involves the expenditure of at least " the price of a pint," and, in the circumstances, this extravagance is not allowable. The guard-room is unwontedly empty—nobody except the utterly reckless will get into trouble just now ; for punishment at this season involves the forfeiture of certain privileges, and the incurring of certain penalties, the former specially prized, the latter exceptionally disgusting at this Christmas season.

Slowly the days roll on with anxious expectancy, the coming event forming the one engrossing topic of conversation, alike in barrack-room, in stable, in canteen, and in guard-room. The clever hands of the troop are deep in devising a series of ornamentations for the walls and roof of the common habitation. One fellow spends all his spare time on the top of a table, with a bed on top of that again embellishing the wall above the fireplace with a florid design in a variety of colours, meant to be an exact copy of the device on the regiment's kettle-drums, with the addition of the legend, " A merry Christmas to the old Strawboots," inscribed on a waving scroll below. The skill of another decorator is directed to the clipping of sundry squares of coloured paper into wondrous forms—Prince of Wales' feathers, gorgeous festoons, and the like—with which the gas pendants and the edges of the window-frames are disguised out of their original nakedness and hardness of outline, so as to be almost unrecognisable by the eye of the matter-of-fact barrack-master himself. What is this felonious-looking band up to, these four determined rascals in the forbidden highlows and stable overalls, who go slinking mysteriously out at the back gate just at the gloaming? Are they Fenian sympathisers bound for a secret meeting, or are they deserters making off just at the time when there is the least likelihood of suspicion ? Nay, they are neither ; but, nevertheless, their errand is a nefarious one. Watch at the gate for an hour, and you will see them come back again, each man laden with the spoils of the shrubberies,—holly, mistletoe, and evergreens,—ruthlessly plundered under cover of the darkness.

A couple of days before "the day," the sergeant-major enters the barrack-room, a smile playing upon his rubicund features. We all know what his errand is, and he knows right well that we do; but he cannot refrain from the customary short, patronising harangue, "Our worthy captain—liberal gent, you know—deputed me—what you like for dinner—plumpuddings, of course—a quart of beer a man : make up your minds what you'll have—anything but game and venison;" and so he vanishes, grinning a saturnine grin. The moment is a critical one. We ought to be unanimous. What shall we have? A council of deliberation is constituted on the spot, and proceeds to the discussion of the weighty question. The suggestions are not numerous. The alternative lies between pork and goose. The old soldiers, for some inscrutable reason, go for goose to a man. The recruits have a carnal craving after the flesh of the pig. I did once hear a "carpet-bag"* recruit hesitatingly broach the idea of mutton, but he collapsed ignominiously under the concentrated stare of righteous indignation with which his heterodox suggestion was received. Goose *versus* pork is eagerly debated. As regards quantity, the question is a level one, since the allowance from time immemorial has been a goose or a leg of pork among three men.

At length the point is decided according as old or young soldiers predominate in the room during the evening stable-hour. The sergeant-major is informed of the conclusion arrived at, and in the evening the corporal of each room accompanies him on a marketing

* "Carpet-bag" recruit is the barrack-room appellation of contempt for the young gentleman recruit who joins his regiment *omnibus impedimentis*—who, in fact, brings his baggage with him, to find it, of course, utterly useless.

expedition into the town. Another important duty devolves upon the said corporal in the course of this marketing tour. The "dimmocking bags" have been emptied ; the accumulations in the sergeant-major's hands have been drawn, and the corporal, freighted with the joint savings, has the task of expending the same in beer. In this undertaking he manifests a preternatural astuteness. He is not to be inveigled into giving his order at a public-house,—swipes from the canteen would do as well as that,—nor do the bottled-beer merchants tempt him with their high prices for dubious quality. No, he goes direct to the fountain-head. If there be a brewery in the place, he finds it out, and bestows his order upon it, thus triumphantly securing the pure article at the wholesale price. His purchasing calculation is upon the basis of two gallons per man. If, as is generally the case, the barrack-room he represents contains twelve men, he orders a twenty-four gallon barrel of porter,—always porter ; and if he has a surplus left, he disburses it in the purchase of a bottle or two of spirits, for the behoof of any fair visitors who may haply honour the barrack-room with their presence.

It is Christmas-eve. The evening stable-hour is over, and all hands are merrily engaged in the composition of the puddings ; some stoning fruit, others chopping suet, beating eggs, and so forth. The barrel of beer is in the corner, but it is sacred as the honour of the regiment! Nothing would induce the expectant participants in its contents to broach it before its appointed time shall come. So there is beer instead from the canteen in the tin pails of the barrack-room, and the work of pudding-compounding goes on jovially to the accompaniments of song and jest. Now, there is a fear lest too many fingers in the pudding may spoil it,—lest a multitude of counsellors as to the proportions of ingredients and the process of mixing may be productive of the reverse of safety. But somehow a man with a specialty is always forthcoming, and that specialty is pudding-making. Most likely he has been the butt of the room,—a quiet, quaint, retiring, awkward fellow, who seemed as if he never could do anything right. But he has lit upon his vocation at last—he is a born pudding-maker. He rises with the occasion, and the sheepish "gaby" becomes the knowing practical man; his is now the voice of authority, and his comrades recant on the spot, acknowledge his superiority without a murmur, and perform "kotow" before the once despised man of undeveloped abilities. They pull out their clean towels with alacrity, in response to his demand for pudding-cloths; they run to the canteen enthusiastically for a further supply, on a hint from him that there is a deficiency in the ingredient of allspice. And then he artistically gathers together the corners of the cloths, and ties up the puddings tightly and securely; whereupon a procession is formed to escort them into the cook-house; and there, having consigned them into the depths of the mighty copper, the "man of the time" remains watching the cauldron bubble until morning, a great jorum of beer at his elbow, the ready contribution of his now appreciative comrades.

The hours roll on; and at length, out into the darkness of the barrack-square stalks the trumpeter on duty, and the shrill notes of the *réveille* echo through the stillness of the still, dark night.   On an ordinary morning the *réveille* is practically negatived, and nobody thinks of stirring from between the blankets till the "warning" sounds quarter of an hour before the morning stable-time.   But on this morning there is no slothful skulking in the arms of Morpheus.   Every one jumps up, as if galvanised, at the first note of the *réveille*.   For the fulfilment of a time-honoured custom is looked forward to,—a remnant of the old days when the "women" lived in the corner of the barrack-room. The soldier's wife who has the cleaning of the room, and who does the washing of its inmates,—for which services each man pays her a penny a day,—has from time immemorial taken upon herself the duty of bestowing a "morning," on the Christmas anniversary, upon the men she "does for."   Accordingly, about a quarter to six, she enters the room,—a hard-featured, rough-voiced dame, perhaps, with a fist like a shoulder of mutton,—but a soldier herself to the very core, and with a big, tender heart somewhere about her.   She carries a bottle of whisky—it is always whisky, somehow—in one hand, and a glass in the other ; and beginning with the oldest soldier, administers a caulker to every one in the room, till she comes to the "cruity," upon whom, if he be a pullet-faced, homesick bit of a lad, she may bestow a maternal salute in addition, with the advice to consider the regiment as his mother now, and be a smart soldier and a good lad.

Breakfast is not an institution in any great acceptation in a cavalry regiment on Christmas morning. When the stable-hour is over, a great many of the troopers do not immediately reappear in the barrack-room. Indeed, they do not turn up until long after the coffee is cold ; and, when they do return, there is a certain something about them which, to the experienced observer, demonstrates the fact that, if they have been thirsty, they have not been quenching their drought at the pump. It is a standing puzzle to the uninitiated where the soldier in barracks contrives to obtain drink of a morning. The canteen is rigorously closed. No one is allowed to go out of barracks, and no drink is allowed to come in. A teetotaller's meeting-hall could not appear more rigidly devoid of opportunities for indulgence than does a barrack during the morning. Yet I will venture to say, if you go into any barrack in the three kingdoms, accost any soldier who is not a raw recruit, and offer to pay for a pot of beer, that you will have an instant opportunity afforded you of putting your free-handed design into execution any time after seven A.M. I don't think it would be exactly grateful in me to " split " upon the spots where a drop can be obtained in season ; many a time has my parched throat been thankful for the cooling surreptitious draught, and I refuse to turn upon a benefactor in a dirty way. Therefore, suffice it to say that many a bold dragoon, when he re-enters the barrack-room to get ready for church parade, has a wateriness about the eye, and a knottiness in the tongue, which tell of something stronger than the matutinal coffee. Indeed, when the trumpet sounds which calls the regiment to assemble on the parade-ground, there is dire misgiving in the mind of many a stalwart fellow, who is conscious that his face, as well as his speech, " betrayeth him." But the lynx-eyed men in authority, who another time would be down on a stagger like a card-player on the odd trick, and read a flushed face as a passport to the guard-room, are genially blind this morning ; and, so long as a man possesses the capacity of looking moderately straight to his own front, and of going right about without a flagrant lurch, he is not looked at in a critical spirit on the Christmas church parade. And so the regiment marches off to church, the band play-ing merrily in its front. I much fear there is no very abiding sense in the bosoms of the majority of the sacred errand on which they are bound.

But there are two of the inmates of each room who do not go to church. The clever pudding-maker and a sub of his selection are left to cook the Christmas dinner. This, as regards the exceptional dainties, is done at the barrack-room fire, the cook-house being in use only for the now-despised ration meat and for the still simmering puddings. The handy man cun-ningly improvises a roasting-jack, and erects a screen, consisting of bed-quilts spread on a frame of upright forms, for the purpose of retaining and throwing back the heat. He is a most versatile genius, this handy man. Now we see him in the double character of cook and salamander, and anon he develops a special faculty as a clever table-decorator as well. This latter qualification asserts itself in the face of diffi-culties which would be utterly discomfiting to one of less fertility of resource. There is indeed a large expanse of table in every barrack-room ; but the War Department has not yet thought proper to con-sider private soldiers worthy to enjoy the luxury of table linen. Yet bare boards at a Christmas feast are horribly offensive to the eye of taste. Something must be done; something has already been done. Ever since the last issue of clean sheets, one or two whole-souled fellows have magnanimously abjured these luxuries *pro bono publico.* Spartan-like, they have lain in blankets, and saved their sheets in their pristine cleanliness wherewithal to cover the Christmas table. So now these are brought forth, not snow-white certainly, nor of a damask texture, being indeed somewhat sackclothy in their appearance, but still they are immeasurably in advance of the bare boards; and when the covers are laid, with each man's best knife and fork, with a little additional crockery-ware borrowed of a beneficent married woman, and with the dainty sprigs of evergreen stuck on every available coign, the effect is triumphantly enlivening.

By the time these preparations are complete, the men are back from church; and after a brief attendance at stables to water and feed, they assemble fully dressed in the barrack-room, hungrily silent. The Captain enters the room, and *pro forma* asks whether there are "any complaints?" A chorus of " No, sir," is his reply; and then the oldest soldier in the room, with profuse blushing and stammering, takes up the running, thanks the officer kindly in the name of his comrades for his generosity, and wishes him a "happy Christmas and many of 'em" in return. Under cover of the responsive cheer, the Captain makes his escape, and a deputation visits the Sergeant-major's quarters to fetch the allowance of beer which forms part of the treat. Then all fall to and eat! Ye gods, how they eat! Let the man who affirmed before the Recruiting Commission that the present scale of military rations was liberal enough show himself now, and then for ever hide his head! The troopers seem to have become sudden converts to Carlyle's theory on the eloquence of silence. It reigns supreme, broken only by the rattle of knives and forks, and an occasional gurgle indicative of a man judiciously stratifying the solids and liquids, for a space of about twenty minutes, by which time—be the fare goose or pork—it is, barring the bones, only "a memory of the past." The puddings, turned out of the towels in which they have been boiled, then undergo the brunt of a fierce assault; but the edge of appetite has been blunted by the first course, and with most of the men a modicum of pudding goes on the shelf for supper. The soldier is very sensitive on the subject of his Christmas pudding. I remember once seeing a cook put on the table and formally "strapped" for allowing the pudding to stick to the bottom of the pot for lack of stirring.

At length dinner is over. Beds are drawn up from the sides of the room, so as to form a wide circle of divans round the fire, and the big barrel's time has come at last. A clever hand whips out the bung, draws a pailful, and reinserts the bung till another pailful is wanted, which will be very soon. The pail is placed upon the hearthstone, and its contents are decanted into the pint basins, which do duty in the barrack-room for all purposes, from containing coffee and soup to mixing chrome yellow and pipe-clay water. The married soldiers come dropping in with their wives, for whom the Corporal has a special drop of "something short" stowed in reserve on the shelf

behind his kit. A song is called for; another follows,
and yet another and another. Now it is matter of
notice that the songs of soldiers are never of the
modern music-hall type. You might go into a
hundred barrack-rooms or soldiers' haunts and never
hear such a ditty as "Champagne Charley" or "Not
for Joseph." The soldier takes especial delight in
songs of the sentimental pattern; and even when, for
a brief period, he forsakes the region of sentiment, it
is not to indulge in the outrageously comic, but to
give vent to such sturdy bacchanalian outpourings as
the "Good Rhine Wine," "Old John Barleycorn,"
and "Simon the Cellarer." But these are only inter-
ludes. "The Soldier's Tear," "The White Squall,"
"There came a Tale to England," "Ben Bolt,"
"Shells of the Ocean," and other melodies of a
lugubrious type, are the special favourites of the
barrack-room. I remember once hearing a cockney
recruit attempt the "Perfect Cure," with its accompanying gymnastic efforts; but he was not appreciated, and, indeed, I think broke down in the middle
for want of encouragement.

Songs and beer form the staple of the afternoon's
enjoyment, intermingled with quiet chat consisting
generally of reminiscences of bygone Christmases.
Here and there a couple get together who are
"townies," i.e., natives of the same district; and
there is a good deal of undemonstrative feeling in
the way they talk of the scenes and folks of boyhood. There is no speechifying. Your soldier is
not an oratorical animal. Not but what he heartily
enjoys a speech; but he somehow cannot make one,
or will not try. I remember me, indeed, of a cer-

tain quiet Scotsman, who one Christmas-time being
urgently pressed to sing, and being unblessed with
a tuneful voice, volunteered in utter desperation a
speech instead. He referred in feeling language to
the various troop-mates who had left us since the
preceding Christmas, made a touching allusion to
the happy home circle in which the Christmases of
our boyhood had been spent, referred to the manner
in which the old "Strawboots" had cut their way
to glory through the dense masses of Russian horse-
men on the hillside of Balaclava; and wound up appro-
priately by proposing the toast of "Our noble selves."
He created an immense sensation, was vociferously
applauded, and, indeed, was the hero of the hour;
but ere next Christmas he was among the "have
beens" himself, and his mantle not having devolved
upon any successor, we had to content ourselves with
the songs and the beer.

It is a lucky thing for a good many that there is
no roll-call at the Christmas evening stable-hour.
The non-commissioned officers mercifully limit their
requirements to seeing the horses watered and bedded
down by the most presentable of the roisterers, whose
desperate efforts to simulate abject sobriety in order
to establish their claim for strong-headedness is very
comical to witness. It has often been matter of
wonderment to me how the orders for the following
day, which are "read out" at the evening stable-
hour, are realised on Christmas evening with clear-
ness sufficient to insure their being complied with
next day without a hitch; but the truth is that, as
we shall presently see, a certain order of things for
the morning after Christmas has become stereotyped.

This interruption of the evening stable-hour over, the circle reforms round the fire, and the cask finally becomes a "dead marine." The cap is then sent round for contributions towards a further instalment of the foundation of conviviality, which is fetched from the canteen or the sergeants' mess; and another and yet another supply is sent for as long as the funds hold out and somebody keeps sober enough to act as Ganymede. The orderly-sergeant is not very particular to-night about his watch-setting report, for he knows that not many have the physical ability to be absent if they were ever so eager. And so the lights go out; the sun of the dragoon may be said to set in beer, and he is left to do his best to sleep himself sober. For in the morning the reins of discipline are tightened again. The man who is foolish enough to revivify the drink which "is dying out in him" by a refresher, is apt to find himself an inmate of the black-hole, on very scant warning. Headaches and thirst are curiously rife, and the consumption of "fizzers,"—a temperance beverage of an effervescent character, vended by an individual with the profoundest trust in human nature on the subject of deferred payments, is extensive enough to convert the regiment into a series of walking reservoirs of carbonic acid gas. The authorities display a demoniacal ingenuity in working the beer out of the system of the dragoon. The morning duty on the day following Christmas is invariably " watering order with numnahs," the numnah being a felt saddle-cloth without stirrups. Every man, without exception, rides out—no dodging is permitted—and the moment the malicious fiend of an orderly-officer gets clear of the barracks, he gives the word "Trot!" Six miles of it, without a break, is the set allowance; and it beats vinegar, pickles, tea smoked in a tobacco-pipe, or any other nostrum, as an effectual generator of sobriety. Six miles at the full trot, without stirrups, on a rough horse, I can conscientiously recommend to the inebriated gentleman who fears to encounter a justly irate wife at two in the morning. I won't answer for the integrity of his cuticle when it is over; but I will stake my existence on the abject profundity of his sobriety. The process would extract the alcohol from a cask of spirits of wine, let alone dispel an average skinful of beer.

And thus evaporates the last vestige of the dragoon's Christmas festivity. It may be urged that the enjoyments of which I have endeavoured to give a faithful narrative are gross, and have no elevating tendency. I fear the men of the spur and sabre must bow to the justice of the criticism; and I know of nothing to advance in mitigation save the old Scotch proverb, "It is ill to mak' a silk purse out o' a sow's ear."

CHRISTMAS IN THE FOREPOSTS,
1870.

CHRISTMAS IN THE FOREPOSTS, 1870.

IT was Christmas morning *vor Paris.* Where shall we dine? I know where I should have liked to dine; but the obstinate Parisians came between one and "the old folks at home," and the young ones as well. I had no need to complain of want of Christmas invitations; it was in their very number that the bewilderment lay. I refrain from more than an allusion to one kind invitation from one who was ever kind. Then there was that genial one from compatriots in Versailles. Good old Dr Tegener, of the Ecouen Hospital, had sent round another, with a postscript to the note in the shape of the single word " Punch." Some merry lads in Epinay wished me to go down there, and be jovial under the shadow of La Briche; a battery of artillery would be glad of my company —at least they said so—at Napoléon-St-Leu; a battalion of Würtembergers in Champs had half booked me more than a fortnight before; and the list ended with the genial and cordial invitation of good Major von Schönberg and his officers, of the 2d battalion of the 103d Saxon regiment. It was the battalion's turn on Christmas night for duty on certain far outlying oreposts in front of the village of Raincy. The

officers I knew to be right hearty fellows; then there
was Frau Majorin's Bavarian beer (per Feldpost).
Yes, I said done and done again with the major.   It
was a long ride, with the temperature, too, below
freezing-point, and things over on the French side
were not altogether tranquil; but the way I was going
would bring me to the right spot, if that sluggish firing from the forts should warm up and cover a sortie.

I arrive at the château in Clichy, and put up my
horse there, going out to the advanced foreposts
before the day fades.   As I reach the garden opening into the forest, a discouraging sight meets the
eye.   Four soldiers are carrying on their shoulders a
motionless form, lying on a stretcher, and covered
with a bloody blanket.   " Wounded ?"   The solemn
" Dead " comes from the mouth of the accompanying
under-officer.   It is a corpse they are carrying up
into the village.   This was Private Jeskow's last
Christmas morning.   He was making his coffee in a
house behind outpost No. 8, when a shell burst under
the window.   His sergeant told him he was in dangerous quarters, but the coffee was near the boil.
Before it boiled, another shell had come and burst in
the room ; a fragment struck Jeskow in the back, and
killed him.

Forward down a slope through a solitary wood of
dense underwood, mingled with goodly trees.   On
the pathway are numerous craters of shells.   There
is a little rise, and then I emerge on to a belt of
healthy clearing in the wood.   Everywhere the wood
has been full of barricades, of *chevaux de frise* of
all kinds of appliances for arresting an enemy.   On
this cleared belt are works of greater pretension—

parallels, entrenchments, strong stockades, trenches, enfiladed approaches, and what not. A few soldiers were visible about it. There are more among the huts to the right. What a glorious sky is that which lies over the faint gossamer-like smoke of Paris. The sun is going down, not in human blood this Christmas afternoon, but in blood-like hues of his own creation. All the firmament is rippled in crimson wavelets, and the light comes ruddy on the earth, as if it fell through stained-glass windows. Five minutes brings one across the clearing into more scrub, and then into a village of châteaux nestling in the scrub. Forest, clearance, and village all reminded me very much of the neighbourhood of Chislehurst in Kent. There is the same ruggedness, and still the same appearance of vicinity to the Metropolis, in the physical aspect of the scene.

On the cross-roads, in the centre of this collection of villages, I meet the officers in command of the two battalions waiting to be relieved. The men are massed behind the walls. They are sauntering up and down on the exposed road. Any news? None. Perhaps a little. At ten o'clock this morning two French brigades had deployed in parade order before Bondy in two long lines. Then it seemed as if the troops marched past a general, and formed a hollow square, in which they stood for nearly an hour, after which one brigade went back to quarters, while the other marched on to the foreposts. It was conjectured that a religious service was being performed while the troops stood there in hollow square. If so, Du Nord and De l'Est furnished the responses, for they were firing at that hour. About the same hour three brigades were visible, marching in the front of Aubervilliers; and the observatory officer reported that he had seen two naval batteries arrive by train at Bondy, and immediately push forward, as if to take up position. This would seem to argue that there were to be heavy batteries so near as Bondy, which must, it seemed, in the event of their not being shut up by our still, grim, silent friends that sulked behind the parapets in our rear, have the inevitable result of widening the circle of our forepost environment.

Tramp, tramp, tramp, here comes the 103d. There is the major in front talking earnestly with the field-officer he is going to relieve. Here comes Hammerstein, unrecognisable by reason of wraps, and only to be discerned and greeted by his voice. He has got on a pair of fur boats, that seem a legacy from an Esquimaux, and here is his big brother-in-law, Kirchbach, and von Zanthier, and the whole lot of them. Now comes the relieving of the foreposts—a ticklish duty, for the relief must be in full possession before the relieved dare to come out. As each company goes on to its post, it is met by a trusty non-commissioned officer of the departing outpost, who acts as its cicerone. Then the sergeant and the lieutenant go out and change the sentries, and, with a cheery "Good night," off stumps the "old guard." Glad enough to go, beyond doubt. The duty here just now is one night on, one night off; but when, as has occurred for the last three days, the day and night "off" are spent standing on the alert, there is not much relaxation. Two battalions, instead of one, are now detailed for the outposts, owing to the necessity for dry-nursing in this way the babes in the wood, who have not yet begun to squall; and this makes the duty all the harder.

The relieving duty over, we reach our home for the night out beyond the villas. Let me describe it. It is a long, low, wooden hut, such as you may see squatters and gipsies occupying on the debatable ground between Peckham, Lewisham, and Nunhead Cemetery. Its loftiest part is about six feet high, the roof sloping till, at the back, the height is about four feet. The erection is wholly of wood—chiefly, as it appears, of château doors. There is one window in the place; it is sashed, and tastefully curtained. There is a wooden floor. One—the lower-roofed side of the room—is lined with spring mattresses, that have evidently also come out of the châteaux. On the walls are pictures—aye, and mirrors—to be ascribed to the same origin; and between the window and the beds is a range of good massive mahogany tables, that were not made by the pioneers. The chairs are a study. They are here of all styles; the fauteuil, the ottoman, the American rocking-chair, the high straight-backed Elizabethan, the Louis Quatorze settee, and the humble wicker-bottom. There is a pleasant fire burning in the little stove, and you cannot well imagine how cheerful, with the bright lamp burning and the sparkle of the fire, the little nest looked—if you could only forget that the French were not 1000 yards off, and that you were in so ludicrously easy range of their guns.

But we did forget these facts somehow. The quarters were those of a Hauptmann, he in whose charge

Q

was the uttermost forepost.   But by common consent
the officers from the other positions further back—
the *repli*, where the major had his post, and the captains from the right and left rear, came dropping in
to eat their Christmas dinner with the English guest
and comrade.   The kitchen was a part of the hut
partitioned off, and we had the battalion cook there
—a resplendent being in a white cap and apron.
Before dinner he entered in state and lit the candles
on the Christmas-tree, a goodly sprout, from every
bough of which dangled cakes and comfits.   The
cloth—we had a cloth, never mind about its colour—
was laid, the plates and wine were warmed, and we
drew around the social board.   I am in a position
to present the reader with the Christmas *menu* of
the 2d battalion of the 103d regiment on the
foreposts: Soup—Liebig's extract ; fish—sardines,
caviare ; entrées—goose sausage, ham sausage, a
variety of undistinguishable sausage ; pièces de ré-
sistance—boiled beef and maccaroni, roast mutton,
and potato salad ; divertissements—schinken, com-
pot of pears, ditto of apples, preserved sour krout ;
cheese, fresh butter, fruit, nuts, biscuits, tarts, &c.
The potables were as follows :—One barrel of Frau
Majorin's beer still to the good, the other a dead
marine ; very good red wine, champagne iced—a
little too much, in fact.   The caterer had stuck the
bottles outside on his first arrival, and it seemed as if
the wine had frozen in a solid mass.   When it came
to be poured out, it would not run.   A proposition
was made that the bottles should be broken, a hatchet
fetched, and a portion of champagne-ice be served
out to each person ; but an officer of an inquiring

turn of mind, who had been pricking the ice on the surface of one bottle with a skewer, found that it was only about half-an-inch thick, and that below there lay a limpid pint of liquid champagne. We pricked all the bottles with the skewer, and got on beautifully.

After dinner there were but two toasts. One was "The King of Saxony;" the other, "Frau Majorin von Schönberg." Both were drunk with enthusiasm; the latter—in her beer—with positive effusion. Then we got to song-singing. A Degenfähnrich came to the front in this line—the young Baron von Zehman. Instrumental accompaniments were forbidden on account of the proximity of the enemy, but the choruses were loud enough to raise the dead, let alone the Frenchmen. Let me give a list of a few of the songs; they deserve popularity in England.

> "Stehe ich in finsterer Mitternacht."
> (Standing in the dark night.)
>
> "Wer will unter die Soldaten?"
> (Who 'll be a soldier?)

The beautiful and plaintive—

> "Ich hatte einen Kameraden,
> Einen besseren findest du nicht."
>
> (I had a comrade,
> A better one ne'er you 'd find.)

I seem to have a hazy notion that somebody tried "Bonnie Dundee," and failed ignominiously.

About ten o'clock a deserter was brought in—a decidedly unfavourable specimen of the French line. He was very dirty, and he had no buttons anywhere —rather a common want I have noticed with French soldiers. He said he was hungry and thirsty. The

major gave him something to eat and the run of a
bottle of brandy, while we listened to the rascal's
lies. When he had finished his rigmarole, which
consisted of all sorts of canards, it was too late discovered that he was as drunk as David's sow. He
insisted on singing the Marseillaise, and when that
was done, roared "*A bas les Prussiens !*" What was
to be done with the wretch ? If he were turned out-
of-doors he would go to sleep in the ditch, and freeze
so hard before morning that you could chip pieces
off him. Ultimately he was relegated to the stable
by the *repli,* where stood the battalion horses, and
was borne away shoulder high, roaring *Vive la
république !*

Enter Under-officer Schultz, wooden as ever, a
little woodener perhaps on account of the hard frost.
Under-officer Schultz came to read the orders. Ordinarily he would have read them dry and gone away
dry ; but this was Christmas-time, and kindliness
prompted the wetting of Under-officer Schultz' throat.
" Champagne, red wine, or cognac, Schultz ? " " Cognac, Herr Hauptmann," came woodenly from the lips
of Schultz. Schultz bolted a big glass of cognac, and
then read the orders. I think the cognac gave him
unction to roll out sonorously the sentences of King
Wilhelm's address to his troops, which was in the
orders for the night. Then he went about with a
wooden click of his heels, and disappeared.

Continually there was a circulation of officers as
we sat by the board in the wooden house. The
major and myself were the only sedentaries. Duty
called, and men obeyed it. About midnight Hauptmann von Zanthier rose and buckled on his sword.

He was going round with the patrol; would I go with him? Certainly. There were the officer, three men, and myself. Out we went into the brushwood beyond any of our posts. There were the French outposts—not 500 yards off. We could see the fires lit by the watches. Could a neutral go across and have a chat with them? Well, not exactly; there were two or three obstacles. Here is a noise in the brushwood; somebody is coming down the path; there are three men. A voice says, " *Venez, Messieurs!* " It is a French patrol, and the officer thinks our patrol is French too. Von Zanthier and his men accept the invitation. I stand fast. Presently he comes back with three prisoners—a Mobile officer and two men. The officer is a thorough gentleman. On our way back to the Feldwacht he has an immense deal to say, *de omnibus rebus et quibusdam aliis.* When we get back we find that that wonderful man in the white cap has made egg-flip for us. The Mobile officer joins us heartily in a caulker, and does not need to be pressed to take a little supper. He is a jewel of a man. He tells me he once had a moor in Scotland. He laughs at the notion of Paris capitulating. The Mobiles alone are capable of averting that fate. They certainly are not very brilliant specimens, the two he has met with; but then, as he says, "they were selected promiscuously." More egg-flip, and then the spring mattresses.

WORKHOUSE CHRISTMAS
DEPRAVITY, 1871.

WORKHOUSE CHRISTMAS DEPRAVITY, 1871.

LAST Christmas morning I happened to look in upon my friend Hardknut. Hardknut is of the grocer persuasion ; he is a strongly pronounced political economist of the pitiless school, and may be described as Brutus, Cassius, the typical hard-hearted vestryman, and the skipper of a Yankee emigrant liner rolled into one ; with the additional characteristic that he sands his sugar. I found Hardknut in his back shop and in a fearfully bad temper. " Blow Christmas, I say," he burst out, " here I am, forced to lose two business days. I don't mind Christmas-day so much, but to have to close on Boxing-day as well is too bad. Look at that young rascal of a shop-boy— he had the cheek to ask for a holiday. I 'll work him too hours later for his impudence. And there 's Jemima Ann "—Jemima Ann is Hardknut's wife, and he is henpecked—" she has been reading some rubbish written by some feller called Dickens about Crickets on the hearthstone, and Chimes, and so forth, and she has been sticking holly all over the place, and means to keep Christmas in what she calls the genuine English way. She 's a-seeing to the puddens now. Yah ! I 'm disgusted at the whole concern. There's these idiots that call themselves waits; they came under my window last night, and howled fit to give you the nightmare; and when I got up and shied lumps of coal at them out of window, they abused me for a poor-hearted brute. I'd have had them locked up for a nuisance if the policeman had been handy. You newspaper fellers—you're worse than anybody; publishing long lists of 'special appeals to Christmas charity!' I call it regular imposition, I do. Soft-hearted people read 'em, and give away all their spare cash, and have none to spend with honest hard-working tradesmen like myself. Why, there's Jemima Ann herself has been overcome, and been bleeding me of a fiver to send to some Christmas-dinner fund for juvenile mudlarks, or something of the kind, as if I wasn't paying close on 5s. in the pound of poor's-rates already. I tell you I'm downright sick of the world!"

Having blown the steam off, Hardknut somewhat recovered his equanimity, to which happy end contributed not a little a grim rehearsal of the answer he meant to give the postman and dustman when they should call this morning for their Christmas-boxes. For Hardknut sets his face, "on principle," against Christmas-boxes to the full as strongly as he does against paupers and mendicants in general. He protests emphatically against the necessity of paupers at all; and, lashed into fury by the whip of the growing poor's-rates, enunciates in effect the dictum that if people cannot earn a livelihood by working for it, as he does, they ought to starve contentedly and without any fuss about it. In order to gather a stock of resignation for Jemima Ann's Christmas feast, he

proposed a forenoon visit to St Pancras Workhouse.
"The guardians there," said he, "are men after my
own heart, if the newspapers have not belied them.
They don't value paupers' comfort a ha'porth, and
why should they? What right has a pauper to object
to rats, or to grumble about an atmosphere which he
likens to the Black Hole of Calcutta? No Christmas
nonsense at St Pancras, I warrant you—the regular
skilly and toke, and none too much of that!"

On our way to St Pancras it soothed Hardknut
considerably to observe the policemen on duty, and
thus deprived of the opportunity of making merry on
the absurd festival. It also rejoiced his soul to watch
the omnibuses, and to dwell exultingly on the fact
that the drivers and conductors would be on the road
till late at night. He became quite jubilant as we
passed several bakehouses where "Christmas-day
bakings" were being taken in, the journeymen of
these establishments being thus debarred from join-
ing the giddy throng on the pavement. And Hardknut positively gloated over the frequent spectacle of
male parents carrying the most youthful of their
progeny, while the mother, generally in a new bonnet,
walked alongside. "There's a lord of the creation
for you!" he cried, as rather a limp gentleman went
by carrying a babe on either arm. "He looks uncommon like holiday-making, don't he?" remarked
Hardknut, with a well developed *risus sardonicus*—
"why, the fellow ought to be working to keep his
brats off the parish, and not shambling out there
waiting for the public-houses to open."

But Hardknut contrived to restrain his feelings considerably in view of the treat which he anticipated was

awaiting him in St Pancras Workhouse. He passed
through the lodge quite as if he owned the fee-simple
of the structure ; for Hardknut is a ratepayer, and he
knows it. On the little lawn outside the main entrance
we observed a fountain overhung with weeping ash-
trees, and this totally needless and superfluous amenity
set Hardknut grumbling again. The aspect of the
lobby did not improve his temper. It was profusely
decorated with evergreens ; on the walls hung pretty
chaplets, and green festoons interlaced with the hanging gasclier. "More folly here !" growled Hardknut ;
but he consoled himself with the observation that the
effect was somewhat spoiled by some leakage on the
ceiling. The chapel made him worse, decorated as it
was, to use his expression, "regardless of expense."
While sympathising with my afflicted friend, I could
not but admire the tastefulness of the adornments of
the chapel, simple as they were. Evergreens and
chrysanthemums, with a few embroidered texts, and
an altar-cloth which, I was told, was a present from
the chaplain, comprised the whole materials, but
neatness and taste made the effect go a long way.

It was pitiable to see Hardknut in the kitchen, which
we next visited. He made a rush on entering to one
of a range of great coppers near, expecting, no doubt,
to witness the skilly slowly simmering into perfection,
and he recoiled as if he had been shot when an obvious plum-pudding in a tin and cloth bobbed up to
the surface of the boiling fluid. He rallied, however,
sufficiently to approach the head cook, who, in white
suit and cap as spotless as the attire of the *maître de
cuisine* of a club, was superintending the labours of a
small army of equally spotless subordinates. Before

each stood a great joint of prime roast meat, the rich gravy oozing from its pores on to the platter, and with keen knives and dexterous strokes the white-clad men were cutting the meat up into portions for those wards most adjacent to the kitchen. Others were completing the messes by the addition of pota-toes bursting from their jackets with floury fissures; and yet others were transferring the mess platters into covered metal trays, with hot water linings, to keep the food hot till it should reach the consumer. " Joints, not stickings," I heard Hardknut remark to him-self with an audible groan.   I pitied him as the cook, with conscious pride, led us to a great table, scrubbed snow-white, on which stood a seemingly countless number of tall, cylindrical shapes of considerable size. " All plum-puddings, every one of 'em," quoth the cook, patting complacently the side of a shape— " ninety-three puddings you see here, gentlemen, each one twenty pound weight.   Have a bit?" and he whipped off a shape, cut a lump out of one of the puddings, and pressed it upon Hardknut, who re-ceived it with a kind of blank stolidity of horror.

The cook evidently read the expression of Hard-knut's face as a complimentary tribute from one accustomed only to small things, and he proceeded ruthlessly to pile on the agony—" I 'll give you," he continued, "the receipt for the Pancras pudding, and you can take it home and recommend it to your good lady.   It suits a large family best.   2¼ sacks of flour, 2¼ cwt. of raisins, 2¼ cwt. of currants, 420 lbs. of suet, 50 lbs. of candied peel, 2 cwt. of sugar, 1320 eggs, 14 gallons of old ale, 20 lbs. of citron, and 1 lb. spice.   Put a piece in your pocket, sir, and try it against your own pudding at home. We don't fear competition, sir." Hardknut was utterly dumfoundered. He. put the proffered hunk of fragrant pudding in the tail pocket of his coat, backed vaguely toward a window seat, and sat down all of a heap, obviously on the pudding.

Then the cook spared me a morsel of his attention to tell me that the Pancras Christmas dinner for a grown up person was 6 oz. of roast beef free from bone— "There it is, sir ; no mistake about it "—8 oz. of potatoes, and one pound of the plum-pudding that had extinguished Hardknut, besides a pint of stout, with tobacco and snuff to follow, and fruit and sweets for the women and children, "leastways for such of the women as don't use tobacco." Then the cook took me a tour round the kitchen to point out the great joints roasting before a fire that might have swallowed up several yule logs at once, the scrupulous cleanliness of everything, and the arrangements for securing at once good and economical cookery. As we passed Hardknut, I overheard him muttering, " Plum-pudding for paupers ! "—" Guardians get their groceries from that rascal Scroggins ! "—" To-day's worth another farthing at least on the rates ! "—" I 'll expose sich goings on ! " and such like self-communings. But it was evident that the cook considered that my companion was lost in awe-stricken admiration of what he saw, and he proceeded still further to stun him. " Pancras is equal to more than plum-pudding, sir ; a pudding can be made, but a poet must be born. And we keep a born poet, sir, that we do. Look at one of his poems over the fireplace there :—

Hail, Guardians ! who secure the poor
    Peace, rest, and comfort here ;
May every earthly blessing pure
    Be theirs throughout the year.

Hail, Master ! health, long life, and peace
    Be thine, say one and all ;
Hail, Matron ! may thy joys increase,
    And blessings on thee fall !

There, sir," exclaimed the *chef,* when he had recited
the above, *ore rotundo,* "what do you think of the
Pancras' poet laureate?"   I was truly sorry for poor
Hardknut's torture, and was glad to suggest to him
that as the master, Mr Goodson, with a number
of the guardians and visitors, were going to visit the
various rooms, we might accompany them.

    Our first visit was paid to what are called the
"female lunatic" wards.   Certainly nobody therein
was lunatic enough not to appreciate a good dinner.
The tables were laid with clean table-cloths, and
knives and forks, and the roofs and walls were
thickly hung with pictures, as well as with decorations of evergreens and plenteous festoons of coloured
tissue paper.   Hardknut groaned as he witnessed
these tokens of consideration for paupers; but the
combative spirit was dead within him as when he
encountered the biting tongue of Jemima Ann.   One
lady of the lunatics, the rest of whom were perfectly
sedate and in a state of rigid composure, entered
a formal complaint addressed to the whole collective
Board of Guardians as well as the Local Government
Board, to the effect that the pudding was reprehen-
sively late, and demanded that therefore somebody
should be handed over to condign punishment.   An-

other old lady, blind, white-haired, and aged 88, having shaken hands very effusively with the master, launched forth into copious reminiscences of bygone Christmases. Once, as she told with befitting indignation, the Christmas dinners had been served cold, and without beer. Beer was evidently with her the question of the day; and when the master assured her that the allowance was a pint of stout, the old lady blessed everybody all round, and then burst into a song of thanksgiving. The lady in charge told how the sprightly old creature still nourished hopes of being married, nor did the latter, although she simpered bashfully, deny the soft impeachment.

Christmas-day in the padded room! There is a theme for the writers in the annuals! But yesterday the doors of the padded rooms stood open without exception, and no poor creature, either male or female, required sequestration from the companionship of fellow unfortunates. In the "male lunatic" wards there were but few inmates; but here we found as sturdy a stickler for principle as Hardknut himself. "No compromise" was written in his stern countenance and bushy, black eyebrows. "It is my duty, sir," said he, "to report that we have had only half-a-pint of beer. I do not speak for myself, sir; in fact, I would as soon have no beer at all. One Christmas-day I walked thirty-seven miles from Woolich and back without halting, and never saw beer. But I owe it to my fellows, who have never walked to Woolich and back without beer, to represent the fact that we have had only half-a-pint." It seems the restricted allowance was by the doctor's orders, but the stern man could not be persuaded of this. He took a very high tone

with us, announced himself as Sir Robert Gorham, of
Woolwich Common and Greenwich Park, Bart., and
asserted that he had been gratuitously insulted all
round, especially by Hardknut, on whom he seemed
disposed to fix a quarrel.

Bidding a respectful adieu to the irate baronet,
who continued to fulminate while we were within
hearing, we crossed a court to another region, that
inhabited by the old men.   There are, it may be remarked, more than 900 old men and women over 70
years of age in St Pancras Workhouse. A very
cheerful and pleasant apartment is the day-room for
such ancient gentlemen as are hale enough to quit
the wards in which they sleep. As in all the others,
there are many pictures, the walls and ceiling are
festooned with Christmas decorations, nor are there
wanting books and newspapers. The old fellows with
their beer were sitting round the great, cheery fire-
places, and I rather think that our entrance inter-
rupted a chorus. What was the meaning of the
sombreness in this the next ward that we entered?
An old man pointed silently with his forefinger to
the screens drawn round a cot about half-way down
the ward. One of the old men had not stayed long
enough in the world to eat his Christmas dinner and
drink his Christmas beer ; he had started on the long
journey in the forenoon, and the body lay on the cot
behind the screens till the doctor, then on his rounds
among the living, should formally sanction the removal of the dead.

Some of these old men have known strange
vicissitudes. Who among us can challenge fortune with sufficient assurance that the workhouse

R

be not his lot before he goes to the grave? Ask this venerable gentleman, in long past days a solicitor in large practice, whether in his days of prosperity he would not have laughed you to scorn had you ventured to foretell he would find an asylum in the workhouse in the winter of his days. But here he is, and very eager for the advent of his pound of plum-pudding. Old playgoers will readily remember Huggings, the successor of Emery and Knight in the part of Zeky Homespun in the *Heir at Law*, on the boards of Old Drury. Can they bring themselves to believe that Huggings had sunk to spend his Christmas by the fireside in a ward in St Pancras Workhouse? There was a stoical gallantry of resignation in the bearing of the old broken actor. He has nothing to complain of, he says, in bodily wants; but the want of congenial society bears very hard upon him. A man of real culture—after quitting the stage a lecturer on abstruse scientific topics, and with an intellect still keen and active, he longs with a melancholy eagerness for some congenial converse, and for books on subjects that were wont to interest him in other days. We find old men in the famous "Rat Ward," and in the not less famous "Black Hole of Calcutta." Whatever once may have been, there are no rats now in the cheerful, gaily-decorated room, with which so much scandal has been connected; and the ventilation in the "Black Hole" is as sweet as need be desired. In the latter there lies a boy among the old men—a fragile, dying creature, with worn limbs, and face as of an angel. He has no business here, strictly speaking, but somehow he was placed here on his first admission months ago; and the nurse and

the old men pleaded so hard that he should be left
with them, that nobody has had the heart to remove
him.

A few steps across a court brought us to the nur-
sery wards. The nursing mothers were dining, most
of them, with their babies in their arms. It is a
sinful world this of ours, in which there are to the
full as many sinned against as sinning. It is best,
says the master, not to ask any questions about
these little ones. To quote his own homely phrase,
"They haven't much to brag about in the way of
fathers." Never a one of them has been born in
lawful wedlock, and about some of the mothers there
seems no great stock of virtue outside the virtue of
maternal love. Not a few are acting as foster mothers
to infants deserted by their mothers, in addition to
nursing their own ; and any one not made acquainted
with this circumstance might imagine that twins were
extremely common occurrences among the St Pancras
poor.

In an adjoining ward were the children old
enough to leave their mothers—most of them, in sad
truth, left by their mothers. On low forms round the
hearth sat the solemn, tiny creatures, gravely staring
into the glowing fire with an aspect, spite of their
healthy chubbiness, of premature old age. They sat
there with just the same expression we had noticed
among the old men, through whose wards we had
previously passed, pondering apparently with a queer
weird sagacity upon the anomalies of this world.
Somehow Hardknut, who had hitherto been walking
round an embodied protestation, thawed at the sight
of these infants—it was only a few months ago that

he buried a little chap of his own.   Would you believe
that there were lollipops in the stern man's pocket,
and that he could find it in his heart to kiss a " pauper
brat."

There were many more wards to traverse, but to
write of them at length would only weary the reader.
Suffice it to say, that Christmas decorations, cleanliness, good cheer, and contentment were the characteristics of all, and that it is evident that Christmas,
spite of such men as Hardknut (whose bark, I
honestly believe, is worse than his bite), is evidently
the grand white stone of the year on the sombre
pathway of the pauper.

CHRISTMAS-EVE AMONG THE BEGGARS.

A NEW era is dawning on our Metropolitan pauper-
ism. The sordid and narrow-minded principle is being
acted upon, that we should not bestow our charity
indiscriminately, and without investigation, but con-
form to a system under which applicants are to be
put to the reprehensible inconvenience of standing
the test of a preliminary inquiry into their claims to
be held fitting objects of relief. The title under
which this repulsive engine is known is the Society
for Organising Charitable Relief, and its stoker is Mr
Alsager Hay Hill. It has been at work in Blackheath, St George's, Hanover Square, and Maryle-
bone; while Kensington, Westminster, and Islington
are making arrangements for its introduction within
their respective bounds. The public has been assured that where it has been in operation it has
worked well, that the devices of importers have been
frustrated, and that while none really deserving of
relief have been sent empty away, the fortunate dis-
tricts have been all but cleared of the professional
beggar nuisance. But while there seems to be a *consensus* of opinion that the organisation referred to is
a great success, it may be pointed out that there is a

class deeply interested in the matter, whose views respecting it are wanted to make the *consensus* complete.

Surely the professional beggars themselves, as being deeply interested in the matter, are entitled to have a voice; and I regret to state that they are intensely disgusted with the machinery of the organisation, and are very despondent as to the future prospects of their professional career, in the apprehension of its becoming permanent and general. Whether this assurance will be taken to heart by Mr Hill and his coadjutors I know not; but it is a serious responsibility which they are encountering, in wantonly blighting the prospects of a large number of persons who have hitherto thriven on the credulity and easy good nature of the thoughtlessly charitable. The cadgers are down on their luck, the mumpers are hanging their heads dismally, the canters have lost all enthusiasm in their interesting profession; in short, the whole tribe of professional beggars are spending a very doleful Christmas-tide.

Christmas has been hitherto wont to be a "good time" for the beggar. He has got back to town after his summer tour in the provinces, and, after a temporary period of depression at the dead season, has sprouted forth again into prosperity as the approach of the festive season opens the hearts of the public. He has in London three principal haunts, in the threepenny lodging-houses of which he delighteth to dwell—Wentworth and Fleur de Lis Streets, in Spitalfields; the Mint, Southwark; and the classic neighbourhood of Old Pie, Great Peter, and Orchard Streets, Westminster. When Christmas draweth nigh, he contributes to a joint purse to defray wherewithal the expenses of decorating the common dwelling. Chinese lanterns, festoons of coloured papers, bunches of ribbons, and floral devices in paper flowers are the directions in which his artistic taste develops itself; he is a lover of music, and also of strong drink, hot and sweet.

I had the honour of being present last year at a beggars' Christmas symposium in Whitechapel, at which the ladies and the guests partook of sherry, and a feature of which was a tripe supper. These were good times, and money was rife. One part of the entertainment consisted of a solemn judicial inquiry, conducted by a venerable mumper as judge, assisted by a special jury, the foreman of which was an eminent begging letter-writer, into the nefarious conduct of an individual who had neglected to affix the beggar's "trade mark" to the premises of a wealthy and liberal residenter in the suburbs. The accused was found guilty of the high crime and misdemeanour of treachery to his order, and was fined three half-crowns, which he at once paid, and which were forthwith melted down into gin.

But this Christmas the beggars have neither heart nor funds to make merry as of yore. They have seen the handwriting on the wall, and their hearts have become as water. On Christmas-eve, Westminster, which ere while rang with the sounds of revelry, was drearily silent. Not a stone's-throw from the palatial thoroughfare of Victoria Street, and lying under the shadow of the towers of the palace, are dozens of the low lodging-houses, which are the

chosen haunts of the beggars.   Old Pie Street,
Orchard Street, and Great Peter Street, and the
squalid "Grounds ;" Perkins', Whistler's, and Strutton's,—(who were Perkins, Whistler, and Strutton ?),—
are full of these houses, with their mixed population
of casual labourers, thieves, and beggars.   Notwithstanding the mixture, there is hardly a house but has
a specialty of its own.   One is the chosen haunt of
begging letter-writers ; another is affected almost exclusively by juvenile thieves ; while two or three are
patronised by miscellaneous beggardom.   It was one
of the latter which I visited on Christmas-eve, with a
view to plumb beggar opinion on the Society for
the Organisation of Charitable Relief.   Some half-
dozen broken steps led up to a narrow and dirty
passage, with a crooked descending staircase at the
end of it.   At the foot was a sort of scullery, littered
with refuse, and at the further end a door opened into
the "kitchen," a large, low-roofed room, with dusky
walls, and a huge coke fire burning in the capacious
grate.   There is no better barometer of the condition
of beggardom than the sense of smell.   When fortune smiles, a rich odour of frying pervades the kitchen, and greets you on your entrance.   Pork is the
beggar's dainty ; and if he is thriving, he bends his
energies strenuously on cooking it in one or other of
its various forms.   But no scent of pork fat was
wafted on the breeze as I stumbled down the staircase, nor when I entered was there a solitary supper
in progress.   All round the room there sat forty or
fifty beggars, listless, moody, dispirited, and supper-
less.   Many of them would have been at once recog-

nised by any one familiar with London streets. The
sailor, whose feet have been frosted off, and who
walks on his stumps, was here; the husband, wife,
and five small children, who walk abreast down the
side streets, howling discordantly a hymn tune; the
downcast widow, with the everlasting babe in her
arms; the dilapidated warrior, with his sham oph-
thalmia, and no less sham medals; the patriarchal
gentleman, with two wooden legs; the bull-throated
blind man, who is not blind at all; the pleasant
scrofulous individual, who is always investigating his
sores; several representatives of the interesting class
who go about barefooted on frosty days, with trousers
whose condition is favourable to free ventilation, a
blue-checked shirt, and no other clothing, except
dirt; the paralytic pavement artist, whose *forte* is the
delineation of a mackerel, and several other public
characters. I may remark, that the well-known individual whose legs are tied in a knot, who sits on a
board, and walks on his hands among the feet of his
fellow men, was *not* here. I have heard that he
resides in a freehold cottage in one of the suburbs,
and comes to business every morning in a cab.
There was no judge and jury, no wine, no beer, no
supper even, no joviality, scarcely, indeed, enough
of animation for grumbling. It is true, a forlorn and
half-hearted effort had been made towards the tissue-
paper decorations, of which there were a few festoons
hanging from the roof; but funds or energy had been
lacking to complete the arrangements, and there was
not so much as a Chinese lantern. In one corner
an old blind fiddler fitfully wielded his bow, more,

apparently, from habit than anything else ; but only
the children danced to his strains. They, poor little
wretches, knew not the care which made sombre the
brows of their parents—for them the association had
no terrors. The scrofulous gentleman sounded public
opinion on the subject of beer with the vaguely suggestive remark that he "was wery dry," and was good
for "two browns." But circumstances made the suggestion a barren one—few thought it worth while to
reply at all. One man in the corner said it was all
he could do to raise the price of his bed, and that
beer was not to be thought of; another sarcastically
observed that he had turned teetotaler; and a third
gave vent to the general statement that there was a
tap in the back yard. Just at this juncture, there
entered a short, chubby, comical-looking little Irishman with a crutch, and one of his legs supported by
a sling bandage round his neck. As he proceeded to
divest himself of this totally needless encumbrance,
the man who had avowed himself dry asked him if he
was good for a pot of beer. "Is it beer ye name ?"
replied Barney—"sure wid all the pleasure in life.
There, my honey, just go to the bank, and cash thim
illegant cheques, and bring back the money's worth
in beer ;" and he chucked on the table, with a scorn-
ful sniff, three tickets of the St George's Charitable
Relief Organisation.

The subject of beer faded into insignificance before
the topic suggested by those emblems of the hateful
innovation. Listlessness was exchanged for energy
when the theme was the denunciation of an alteration which had wrought so much dire mischief to the

profession ; and it seemed to be the general opinion, that if the ticket system became general, Othello's occupation was gone. A patriarchal individual, who of a day-time may be seen suffering greatly, to all appearance, from palsy, but whose hands and head were now all right, detailed some interesting experiences about Blackheath, which it appeared had been till lately the theatre of his professional exertions. Blackheath had been a "slap up" district till the fiendish invention of the ticket system ; but of about two hundred and fifty who thrived on its benevolence, he did not believe there were ten now left. He himself had been "jolly well starved out, for how the blazes can a bloke live on tickets ?" he pertinently asked. This discussion had not died out when another man came in, whose experiences, as he related them, illustrate another phase of the suspicious utilitarianism of the times. He was a tall, gaunt Scotsman, with a ragged, grey beard, a baggy Scotch bonnet, a faded tartan waistcoat, and trousers which became rather indefinite below the knee. His branch of the profession was "canting"—*i.e.*, begging from bakers lumps of bread, under pretence of being starving, which he carried away and sold. A large proportion of the bakers of London are Scotsmen, and no doubt he had a good connection among his countrymen, and probably had done tolerably well. But it was clear his equanimity was seriously disturbed. The cause was soon explained.

"Fork out the tommy, Sandy!" "Come, let's have some toke!" "'Arf a brick for me, Sandy!" were some of the exclamations with which he was greeted as he entered.

Sandy stood silent for a space, grimly and sourly surveying his friends. Then with a fierce sniff, as if he were snuffing the wind to add to his wrath, he broke out.

"Tammy! toke! deil a crust have I about me! What think ye, freends? The vera bakers have ta'en to organeese, and be d—— to them. Ye maun be 'drunk on the premises' now, or no get drunk ava'. The first place I gaed to the day, I was aye sure o' my pun' o' bread to tak' awa', forbye a bawbee, or maybe a penny. But thae days are by. He wadna gie me onything, unless I ate it as I stood; and no to mak' a lecar o' mysel', I ate a pun' o' dry bread, an' him standin' lookin' at me. At the next place I was served the same, and so all through the day. I 've eaten four pun' o' bread, and my stamack's blawn oot till I 'm near havin' burstin'."
And Sandy sat down dejectedly, his spirit shrunken if his stomach was distended. His tidings were received with a stolid resignation; the cup seemed so full that a few drops less or more did not much matter. By ten o'clock the company had already been considerably diminished by retirements to the dormitories. To bed at ten o'clock on Christmas Eve! Eheu! *quantum mutatus.*

After leaving the house I have been writing of, I looked into two or three others in which the beggar element is strong. Business was decidedly flat in all of them, all thoughts of the festivities of the season being seemingly merged in brooding over the badness of the times. The begging letter-writers are suffering as much as any of the others, and a cloud was brooding on their ordinarily cheerful and intellectual *coterie*. Something must be done, and that at once, if we would not have our beggars become desperate, and take to honest work, or some such evil course. Surely it cannot seriously be contemplated to exterminate a profession in which so much acumen, plausibility, and mimetic power are engaged.

THE END.